THE LURID SEA

By the Author

Night Sweats: Tales of Homosexual Wonder and Woe

The Lurid Sea

Visit us at www.boldstrokesbooks.com

THE LURID SEA

by

Tom Cardamone

2018

Acknowledgments

Special thanks to my love, my light: Leo, and especially to Len Barot, Cindy Cresap, Craig Gidney, Michael Graves, Trebor Healey, Wayne Hoffman, Sandy Lowe, Melody Pond, Stacia Seaman, Carsen Taite, Ian Titus, Jerry L. Wheeler, and all of the folks at Bold Strokes Books.

Deepest gratitude to Félix Frédéric d'Eon for the use of his fantastic artwork for the cover of this book.

To Boyd McDonald

No rays from the holy heaven come down
On the long night-time of that town:
But light from out the lurid sea
Streams up the turrets silently—

The City in the Sea
Edgar Allan Poe

CHAPTER ONE

A Chariot in the Rain

The hot tub was a frothy mix of foam flecked with miniscule bits of fecal matter, white ribbons of semen and filmy sweat. I basked in this heady broth of hunger and lassitude. Curious feet found mine, quickly recoiled, and returned to tentatively test the ever-so-slight webbing between my toes. All faces were blank. Perspiration coated red brows. A large man edged closer. Dark complexion, black eyes, his thick temple strung with aqueous pearls. Knee to knee, his fingers parted the water toward my erection. I leaned back, head against the slick concrete ledge; I let him trace my silky shaft with the puckered ridges of his waterlogged fingertips. He squeezed and grunted as I exhaled. I dipped my face into the swirling water and thought of the dark currents between the Pillars of Hercules, of the mermen and porpoises cavorting within the deep whorls of the Aegean. I wasn't ready yet to spend my seed, for my hunger bends in a different direction, so I gently backed out of the man's grip. He relented without a word and turned his attention to the young, shallow-chested boy pressed between two older gentlemen. I pivoted, made tiny waves, and rose slowly so that all eyes would be on my supple buttocks as water poured down my back and funneled like a spigot off the curlicue of matted black hair between my legs.

I grabbed one of the damp towels from the nearby rack, wrapped it loosely around my waist, and sauntered down the dim hall. I was in no hurry to discern my whereabouts. What town, what country, even what era, meant little to me. After all, what would I converse with these men about, politics? Here, in the bathhouses across the world, men spoke with their eyes and then their hands, following with silent mouths and other points of entry and egress. And I'm not looking for exits. I live to suck the salt from as many men as possible, giving only a little, to submerge again, in whatever body of water that particular palace holds. Sometimes I part thick cords of pulsing vapor to emerge in another place, as naked as the day I was born. Or at least as naked as the day Neptune cursed me to travel down this road of excess within the aquatic underworld of men who sup on men.

❖

I opened my mouth wantonly and let the towel drop just a bit for a large man within the shadow of a cavernous brick archway. His gaze drilled my form. He beckoned with his chin and turned; I let the towel fall and follow. His shoulders were tense from the hunt, the crevices of his back rolled into a dark gorge of distressed muscle. The threadbare towel cupped his hard buttocks and slapped his thighs. My hunger was a wolf that burrowed into the cave of my throat and dropped a moist litter into my bowels. I *must* feed these squirming pups. His towel dropped. Hands on my shoulders guided me down. His cock wavered before my mouth and, kneeling, my fingers combed the wide swath of pubic hair that swarms his pelvis. My tongue hung out of my mouth in unquestioning gratitude, and he rubbed the head of his cock across my lips. I whimpered with delight, a godling that grovels at the bony feet of men, one who sucks stringy loops of ambrosia from their warm laps and rolls in ecstasy on cold semen-stained cement floors. Invert Mount Olympus into heavenly basements of captured clouds of white roiling steam, disembodied sounds of panting, rough hands and dark corners, and you will find me on the ground, wet pinions of delight smeared across my cheeks. Heaven in Hades, I feasted on his length. I placed his palm on the back of my neck, the better for him to know he was my driver. I was a chariot in the rain, his to ride. I held him in my mouth and throat with an applied rhythm. The man widened his stance. The weak light still somehow reached his blanched toenails. I liked how his toes reflexively pulled at the slimy ground as I increased my speed.

"You're pretty good at this."

I nodded vigorously and disengaged for a moment, cradling the wet cock in one hand, steadying myself with my other hand on the cold concrete floor.

"I've sucked miles of cock."

My momentary partner chortled and, thumb on the glistening head of his dick, impatiently pushed it back down toward my parted lips.

"Well, c'mon now. You've got a million miles to go before you get home."

I could only nod in agreement at this bewilderingly ironic statement, and I dove back onto the shaft. The cock in my mouth was now the single most important organ within my own body. As this second cylindrical heart lay heavy on my tongue, I closed my eyes tight, arms back as if I were about to dive, and dive I did, plunging over and over toward the cliff of muscled crotch—granite against my nose, pubic hair up into my nostrils, and the penis in my mouth exploded, and I fed and swallowed and licked the life-giving testicles in abject gratitude. Bliss and more, as by now other men had gathered around us. Towels dropped and I fed like a blind beggar let out of an infernal prison into the daylight for the first time in eons. These men were my collective sun, each strand of semen deposited into my eager mouth a ray of light. With my every gasp, hands holding calves steady, nodding to the next one, each movement and sound conveyed the same message: paint my tongue white.

This went on forever.

Eventually, the last man shivered and withdrew to spew ropey strands of cum on my cheeks, grunts and shudders as I groveled, and then he exhaled and leaned back against the wall as I licked myself clean. The whimpering wolves caged within my gut curled and stretched with satiated glee.

Chapter Two

This Grateful Serpent

Let's talk about my throat. Once you move past my hospitable lips, that performance called a tongue, there is the throat. I eschew vaginal descriptions. For the most part we are men here, a few glorious creatures are something between a man and a woman and I befriend them, finding their difference a blessing, a relief, proof that we are a flourishing garden and not opposing sides of a duly carved chess board, but I digress. Let's talk about my brother, Obsidio. My brother was the first to discover the congress of my throat. He was big for his age. His feet came in first, huge, always black-soled for he liked to prowl outside our mansion gates at night, as was his nature, his being sired by the God of Death and all that that entails. Black hair, raven-winged but greased for trickery, not flight. He was as stern and stealthy as our mother, enabling him to sneak up on me whenever he liked which, as he was a few years older and matured early, was often. Those sinewy feet looked as if they were formed to climb walls, to hang from the looming branch of a dead tree over some crumbling tomb beside a barren stretch of the Appian Way.

Our house was situated in the heart of Viminal Hill, one of the oldest, wealthiest neighborhoods of Rome. Such illustrious households were centered around an open courtyard with a life-giving fountain. I studied my Grecian scrolls here. See? I was always drawn to water. Whenever Mother went out shopping or banqueted at a friend's mansion, my brother knew where to find me.

Mother. Obsidio inherited all of her darkness, her mercurial moods. We split her ample carnal desire. I took her small frame, my brother her distant eyes. Her desires were endless, exhausting slaves, gods, senators, centurions, priest and priestess, merchants, and assorted freedmen of dubious trades. She took them all in her chambers, some on the library divan, others on the cool marble floor of the vestibule, our ancestral masks staring straight ahead, stoic, eyelessly censorious over the moaning below. Often in full view of us when we were infants. As we grew she became more circumspect, though it's more likely her tastes developed intricacies that required more private ministrations. Either way, we were often alone.

❖

Back to Obsidio.

Just saying his name causes my throat to tighten in the grip of that most wanton of lusts, the familial.

Obsidio.

His name is ash on my tongue. A gray ash smoothed and molded into a paste by the very saliva he summons—a new unguent I apply to every cock I fellate that is not his. No matter the man, *he* is always in my mouth.

Obsidio.

He came upon me silently, as always. A flutter of starlings announced his presence as he batted the scroll out of my small hands and pushed me down into the raked pebbles. His knuckles protruded like pulleys working fine, long fingers.

Soon after his penis lengthened and the blackest hair slithered out of his pores and gathered around its root, he figured out how to mount my young, hairless body from behind one night in an Athenian graveyard while on family holiday. At home, he used his taloned toes like a second pair of hands to better hold me down. He stuffed his balled tunic in my mouth to silence me, the broth of his odor and sweat arousing my initial appetite, as if the cloth were a cork so my dormant skill could ferment as he worked my backside.

I marveled at the length and girth of his penis as mine had yet to sprout. Obsidio grimly charted its emerging growth within the crack of my ass, commenting that soon he would be able to root out my internal organs and I would become an empty vessel, that when he was finished pumping me with semen, he would stand me on my head, plant purple amaranths in my cavity and present me as the centerpiece for our next family banquet. Being ignorant of anatomy, such talk terrorized and thrilled me. I cherished the image of my body as a mere unadorned vase to be filled with random things.

❖

A slave stood solemnly on a ladder trimming the date palms above us as Obsidio was slamming his piece into me one afternoon. At some point, my cries and whinnies proved a distraction to my brother, so he hollered in exasperation, "I've got an idea on how to shut you up."

He flipped me over and spun me round as if I were but a pup, and slapped his steaming cock, greasy from my internal oils, across my lips. Loosening the rag from my mouth, he plunged in.

You would think there would have been at least a moment's resistance to this alien act, a new violation of my immature body. Not at all. I pivoted, and, on all fours, I assumed my intended vocation—no, my reason to exist. Mine was a life of eternal supplication.

Finally, I understood the physical act of prayer.

He gasped as I swallowed his length, tasting his glans as it passed, swabbing the underbelly of his engorged cock as it rode over my tongue and down the fitted funnel of my throat. I reflexively swallowed to pull him in, nose bent upward on his still-bald stomach. His pubic hair was jackal thick, so coarse my gums bled the first few times I sucked his penis, until I adjusted. He swiftly ejaculated. His semen clung to my tongue like gasping fish to a net. I hooked a globule with my finger and held it aloft. It glistened like highly polished onyx.

This was the only physical evidence he was the son of Pluto.

I let the sticky substance swing from my fingertip like a black pendulum. We knew then we were done with the foolish business he was conducting within my ass. My mouth, my throat, was a perfect fit for his cock. It's where it belonged; a living sheath for his scarab.

From then on, until we were separated the night my father cursed me with immortality, we shared his bed. And while he slept, I was nestled between his legs, nursing this grateful serpent.

CHAPTER THREE

The Echo of My Delirium

The ocean of my birth was the secret basement within the marble and brick bowels of the Baths of Caracalla. After my brother both divined and elicited my true nature, my hunger grew insatiable. Yet when he was in one of his increasingly sullen moods, I began to frequent the baths to seek additional succor. This was a natural excursion for a bookish lad, as the baths housed one of the most well-stocked libraries in the city of Rome. Our slave, the incongruously named Perseus, was a shy, silly eunuch whose main duty was the care of my mother's hair, though he was additionally charged with accompanying me whenever I left the house. He enjoyed my trips to the baths, and since he was singularly nearsighted, it was easy to give him the slip.

Once we had settled in at the baths, I liked to wallow, nearly submerged, in one of the heated pools, eyes level with the water, and observe the size and shape of the various organs floating between the legs of the assorted men lounging in the water. I would tuck my own erection between my thighs and set my sights on the tastiest cock. If the owner was interested, I soon learned, he would give the slightest, nearly imperceptible nod and depart for more private quarters, such as an empty massage room or one of the darkened resting areas. All were circumspect, for such escapades with freeborn youth such as myself were taboo, and thus that much more titillating. After several visits to the baths, I worked up the nerve to follow and learned to hone the skills I practiced daily on my brother. Age, girth, nationality, disposition—all meant nothing to me. What I craved hung between their legs and belonged in my mouth. Some patted my head in approval, but others pushed me away once they were spent. The bitter salt of their disdain did not bother me in the least. I was already peering past their thighs toward the next slippery banquette. That was when I became aware of the competition. Other boys and men forded the same ravenous waters. At first, my thirst seemed so singular, so obsessive, that I did not imagine others could possibly share my predilection, did not notice similar assignations within the steam, couplings in the corners, and so on.

❖

Late one evening, after Mother had departed for a fortnight to join in the bacchanalian banquets of a disgraced senator recently exiled to his Tuscan vineyard, I lingered at the baths. Concerning the senator—faint punishment for a notorious drunk, imprisoned within acres of succulent vice. Perseus slept on a bench while I sucked on a centurion for the third time. He had caught my eye in the *frigidarium* and I followed him to the toilet, where I took him in my mouth while he squatted to release his bowels. His thickness was a challenge, though the fact that the rankness of his pubes could not be scrubbed away no matter how many soaks compelled me forward. After I swallowed his globular seed for the first time, he claimed me like a pet and had me follow him from pool to pool, his massive hand always on my neck. The second feeding took place in one of the dark resting chambers, where he jammed a large, calloused toe in my mouth while massaging himself back into full, towering length. Our third session ended in one of the steam rooms. The breadth of him stretched my lips and worked my throat, my own little divining rod pert and quivering as my knees slid slightly on the tile floor. I steadied myself by gripping his burly calves and realized that what I thought was the echo of my delirium was actually an oral chorus. As the swirling steam momentarily subsided, I saw every man seated on the bench to either side of my centurion had his legs spread with the silhouette of a bobbing, servile head between his knees. I marveled. My sense of specialness and singularity wilted, but rebounded with the thought that I was not alone in my taste, that I was among a brotherhood of service, a priesthood swallowing secret sacrifice. The centurion grunted as he again flooded my mouth. I felt his whole body go lax while his member softened between my lips. I slowed my suction as the boy working a tall, lanky bald man beside me fell away in exhaustion. The initial flurry of a snore emanated from the listing warrior above as I gingerly pivoted to catch the tall man's flagging erection. He greedily fed me back into his full length. I stopped only to lap his pendulous balls, and then an impatient finger would tap my shoulder, insistent I return to the main task.

The rotund young man recovered and squatted nearby, his mouth open, offering my tall man a choice. He pulled both our heads together and we lapped at his shaft in unison. This dual action brought him to climax as we competed to devour every drop of semen. The young man signaled his eagerness to suck me as well, but I waved him away. He nodded in complete understanding and moved on to help himself to a new arrival. However, the steam was on the wane, and snoring redoubled throughout the room. Time for me to take my reluctant leave.

❖

Perseus handed me my toga in the changing room. As I dressed, the young man from before came in naked, wet and shivering from a dip in the *frigidarium*. As he toweled himself off, I noticed he kept glancing over at me. Not knowing what to do, I smiled, curious about someone who shared my rapacious predilections. He styled his hair in the oddly endearingly though very outdated Cesarean fashion, though he had no impending baldness to disguise, as far as I could tell.

He shuffled on his sandals next to me and blurted out, "I am studying law."

I could not think of an appropriate response, so I said, "I study anatomy."

Cheeks blossoming, he smiled and tilted his head back toward the steam room. "Then I'll see you in class."

After that, my perspective of the baths changed. No longer did I view myself as a magical nymph afloat within a sea of men. I had competition, friendly or otherwise. Some of my fellow *pathicus* knew each other and some were coldly cordial, while others were fiercely competitive, blocking one another's view of the finer specimens. I discovered a tantalizing range of tastes: men who stole glances at other men's feet, youths who stared at men old enough to be their grandfathers, pert pink erections breaking the surface of green water. Sodomy was a strong thirst for many, one that was more prevalent among certain nationalities, or they were just less circumspect, judging from how friends and colleagues would openly assess the bodies of young athletes while getting massaged or sharing wine. The less discreet cocksuckers, however, were quite a school of sharks. One dandy cruelly tripped another as he rushed out of the swimming pool in a frenzy, hypnotized by the long member wagging between a giant Gaul's legs. This was a world within a world, a cunning, quite secret society of looks, gestures, and asides. A language of glances and silent understanding. So I started paying attention to the graffiti scrawled in the toilet stalls, sheepishly looking for my name, for public praise, banners proclaiming my abilities. There I was surprised to learn that "The slave Perseus, ass no longer tight, sucks and sucks with all his might." A rival, and so close to home! Well, the Baths of Caracalla held men by the hundreds, so there was enough to go around. Every time we visited, I saw the plump student, Publius. By then we had introduced ourselves, him wryly stating that when his parents had named him, little did they know how his mouth would indeed be "public" property someday. I left my heritage unstated. The webbing between my toes tended to recede whenever a large number of mortals were present. We acknowledged each other, briefly chatting, but both of us were focused on our duty—nay, our *purpose*.

❖

One sultry afternoon, hot and rainy, the baths had yet to fill up, though within the first hour, I gleefully consumed the cum of two strapping young blond brothers, who were eager to feed me at the same time. I was cherishing the memory of their dueling swords pushing against my cheeks while soaking in one of the hotter tubs when Publius slipped into the *tepidarium* I occupied.

"So you've had the brothers Califrax. Tasty morsels each. Hard to tell them apart, though I think one of them grunts where the other groans."

At first, I was annoyed he had interrupted my respite, much less with the announcement that I had just eaten from a dish the lawyer-in-training had already licked clean.

"How many times have you had them?" I whispered conspiratorially.

"Only once." He shimmied closer.

"They only ever take to someone once, though I think they bugger each other when they can't find fresh relief. Imagine that, brothers…" I immediately thought of Obsidio, how of every cock I had thus far tasted, his was the one that fit my mouth just so, like a muscle removed from my own body and achingly returned. I blushed and submerged my head under water to wash the thought away. I rose and shook droplets from my hair. Publius was close enough that I could smell watered-down wine on his breath. He glanced down into the pool and stared at the fleshy minnow bouncing between my legs.

"So. Do men do this anywhere else in Rome?" I said, redirecting his eyes to my face.

He blinked and looked back up.

"Yes, all over the place. I went to the Coliseum once, late at night. I heard that willing gladiators would lean against a column if they were interested, but all of the ones I approached wanted money."

"So…"

"So I paid for it!" He laughed and dunked his head under water.

I thought he was going to make another move on me, so I crossed my legs, but he rose instead, spurting water out of his mouth.

"But I like coming here instead. Here if there's no action, at least I get in a good swim."

With that he launched into a leisurely backstroke and I

didn't see him again until we were both on our knees in the steam room, side by side, in fraternal cadence.

❖

Publius and I grew closer over the months. One afternoon, Mother held Perseus back to attend to her before a particularly significant banquet on the Palatine Hill, so I was able to go to the baths unaccompanied. Obsidio never went, as he despised people and found the large, open-air swimming pool especially repellent, as it was a place of sun and exercise. He preferred to watch wrestling or stand in the shadows during slave auctions. At the Baths of Caracalla, while my friend and I were both getting our skin scraped and oiled by masseuses, he casually asked if I was going to attend one of the many festivities held during the evening of Lupercalia. I thought he meant the circuses set up near the open-air markets and told him I had long ago outgrown any interest in trained animals or acrobats. He guffawed.

"I'm talking about a different kind of acrobatics. Surely you've heard of the Fellatiolympics."

I shook my head. My eyelids were heavy with sleep. My face had been pummeled beforehand by quite the variety of cock, so I was ready for a nap.

He shot up and waved the masseuses away.

"By the gods above and below, you don't know what I am talking about, do you? This is *the* event, here, in the chambers beneath the *caldarium*. A contest for all of the best cocksuckers in Rome! Real beauties offer themselves up, the best meat in the city, swinging enormous serpents between their legs and the like, all administered and judged by the high priests of Priapus. The winner is awarded a crown of pearls, naturally."

He looked around conspiratorially and lowered his voice.

"Look, I've never been before, but I'm told the competition is so intense that the heat pouring off the bodies of the participants condenses on the roof and drips down on everyone's heads."

His voice dropped to a whisper.

"It's said that at that point, even the gods cum."

I rolled back over on my stomach, to better conceal my fledgling erection.

❖

After Publius's tale, I left the baths restless, and I ordered my litter to swing by the Coliseum. I hadn't been to the games since I was a young child. My mother despised the rabble and I loved my scrolls, so it had been quite some time since I had stood within its damning shadow. I was impressed and a bit intimidated by the massive structure, made all the more ominous by torchlight in the night.

The panting slaves gladly set the palanquin down, and I alighted onto the dusty road. I could already make out figures lingering between the thick columns. Men are always men, lust a permanent, driving force. A variety of males, including impatient members of the Praetorian Guard, off duty and drunk, all stood beneath the arches, outnumbered by the stooped men groveling for their sex. This cadre came in a variety of ages, sizes, and stations, yet all were equal in their desire to serve. I wove between graffitied columns, marble adorned with etched proclamations of love and curses cast on enemies long dead in every language of the empire. The sweaty shoulders and backs of these soldiers worked quietly to erase said claims of immortality as men moaned beneath them. The sounds of so much sucking and fucking wafted through the Coliseum's antechambers like steady waves lapping the walls of a brackish grotto. Enraptured, I loosened my toga, nearly intent to run naked through the columns, drunk on the noise, the smells of sexual congress, so different from the baths, yet so similar.

Here men gathered in pools of shadow and made their own steam.

A large, broad-shouldered man marched slowly toward me. I could tell he was from the provinces by his bad haircut and oafish sandals. His flat nose betrayed the occupation of a wrestler. His tunic was short. He pulled at the barely concealed bulge beneath it and gave me a hard, cold look, silently commandingly my complete and utter servitude. I demonstratively swallowed, hoping to appear more fearful than I felt, having learned in the baths that some men scoff at the willing while hungry for the demure. I nodded consent with a feigned hesitancy. He turned to the darkness, and I followed. His calves were like melons, his haunches those of a well-worked stallion. I raced after him as he swiveled his head back and forth, searching for a corner to call our own. He stopped beneath a low archway, spread his legs, and lifted his tunic over a wide leather belt. Even in the darkness, I could see his sneer of pride. His cock was that magnificent, an expansive muscle that opened like a giving hand, holding an orb of the most precious, veined porphyry marble, pink and polished. My lips parted involuntarily as I sank to my knees and breathed in his animal musk, nestling my cheek against the lush pubic forest that burst forth around his now-quivering totem. He sighed and relaxed against the wall as I grasped the large, rough big toe of each foot, the better to steady myself. He filled my mouth fully. I choked down his length while teething on the perfect, plump head, a salty effluence already leaking from the puckered tip. His large hand rested atop my skull. Flat, simian fingertips dug into my brow comfortably as he regulated my speed of service. Occasionally, he would pop his penis out of my mouth and slap away the excess saliva across my cheeks. I used such reprieves to gasp for air, correct my position, and swallow hard to better clear the path for re-entry. At one point, his considerable thumb began to stroke my eyebrow as his breathing turned quick and shallow, and I correctly interpreted this to mean he was near release. Just as this thought entered my head, he flooded my mouth with a charge of salty, milky cream, a continuing, forceful surge. I gulped it down as my own little soldier spurted involuntarily on the sand between his legs. He collapsed onto the ground, exhausted. His weight pulled me down and forced my face into the dirty sand, my semen smearing into my closed eyes as I coughed.

He reached out and pulled my toga up across my torso and lightly massaged my ass as cum continued to issue forth from his flagging cock. Sated, he exhaled deeply and sank farther to the ground, his legs extending to either side of my body. A snore issued from out the thick pout of his mouth. I stood, dusted myself off, and left him there to be robbed of whatever paltry coins weighted down his purse.

❖

My body, drunk on sperm and emancipated by sexual exertion, hummed its own song as I made my way through the columns, wondering where my litter had been parked. My slight nipples were erect, my palms sweaty. The sand beneath my feet felt as if it were about to give way, as if I danced within a swirling hourglass, the ground about to open up to exciting escapades. The air was intoxicating, so different from the atmosphere of the baths, with its impounded smells of men and oils, the din of conversation resounding throughout. This was a new playground. One of many. I wondered what other erotic arenas existed throughout the city. Torchlight flickered off the archways above as two drunken youths hung off one another, their disheveled togas soiled with spilt wine, laughing and kissing as they sought deeper shadows. What other alleys and avenues attracted such activities throughout the city? What other locations and erotic secrets had Publius yet to reveal? Better yet, what did he not yet know? I realized this was happening all over the empire. Everywhere men congregated, men fucked, men sucked, men grunted, men sighed. If I ever happened to fancy a certain race, I needed only travel to that corner of the world to satisfy my tastes. What books had been written about my particular practice? Were entire libraries dedicated to vice? A sense of adventure brimmed within. I would branch out, explore, spread my budding wings and make the world mine.

Light-footed, I was practically skipping, I felt so blissful and carefree, when I tripped over the prone body at my feet. I landed forcefully and wrong, knocking the wind out my lungs. I gulped air and flipped over on my back to push myself away from the cold, inert form. I had touched enough clammy, cold flesh to know this wasn't an unconscious drunk or freshly mugged tourist.

This was a dead body.

The lifeless eyes staring back at me belonged to our servant, Perseus.

His blue, parted lips were smeared with a clotting black wax only I could recognize: the mark of Obsidio. What would, at some sad, future point, be called *Pluto's Kiss*.

CHAPTER FOUR

Magic Happens

The locker room was empty. A dank citrine of fog, the lingering stench of bleach and cum assailed my nostrils as I stepped out of the sauna. Two older men in saggy underwear chatted in low voices among the dimpled and oft-painted lockers, their body hair in electric cameo from the red light of the Exit sign. They did every subtle maneuver imaginable to look me over without appearing to look me over. Otherwise, the bathhouse appeared to be nearly deserted.

Full, empty, the midnight frenzy of men and the boys-who-are-just-now-only-men, their furtive steps into the locker room, the loudly dropped keys and embarrassingly hard cocks poking out of fearfully gripped towels low on lanky hips, trapping the sweaty aroma of poorly wiped asses, or the calculating bathhouse veterans, stationed near the door at five o'clock to assess the latest numbers as the after-work crowd streams in. The attendant staff circulates. Tanned and bored shirtless towel boys in tight red shorts with perfect hair stand beside an empty bin, comparing biceps, coveting the fact that they are *being* coveted. They tell their girlfriends when they get home just how sick and perverted some of these men are, how much they miss their girlfriends while they commit drudgery. The boys neglect to inform their girlfriends about how their former high school swim team coach comes to the baths every Saturday. Their version of overtime entails taking turns with ankles in the air, cold whistle grazing hot chest, sly laughter and deep, probing kisses, as if his tongue were trying to reach back into time and reclaim the first time he saw them raise their arms to dive—I value any and all scenarios.

Just as happy to ford vacant halls for a change, I strode naked and sweaty, stretching as I walked, breathing in the stillness. I absorbed the quietude of an abandoned barracks, a place for men absent of men, but their essence remained. Smells, impressions, shadows, all hung like malevolent, rain-soaked capes from invisible hooks.

Walking through the cement halls was like performing a silent ballet. I wanted to skip and launch into a light run, to remain alive and vibrant until the men I require arrived. To run until I danced, danced until I dove off a cliff, returning to the dark ocean of my lineage. Instead, I chose to take a nap. Finding an unlocked cabin with a heap of damp towels, I made a nest. And of course, while I slept, I sucked my thumb.

And dreamt.

Oh, how I dream. Dreams so different from childhood: Those landscapes were traced by fear and literature. The fingerprints of mighty myths, stories told by tutors and slaves, were pressed into my nighttime imagination. The terror of looming adults, thunder and thwarted need informed the nightmares that bubbled up into cries my wet nurse tried to stop with a tired tit. Now my dreams are so much like my waking world that more than once I laughed aloud, disturbing the owner of the cock placed between my sleeping lips. Even when I take a rest, men come to me. I am often woken by the needy caress of a hefty erection nudging about my face. I recall how I had to apply myself with even more zeal than usual to appease that particular fellow, as if my amusement were directed toward him when really, it was the realization that he was a conscious being and not the imaginary feeder of my permanent lust. The surrounding sweaty delirium was so delicious as to seem unreal. Many times, I had to reassert tongue to cock and tighten my hold on the calves before me to reassure these dreamy paramours. And to reassure myself. Conversely, I have woken teething at the very air, lips parted and tongue out, the vivid dream of a scarred and muscled centurion unloading in my throat so real, so physically believable, that I rose mid-swallow to better engulf the imaginary penis stabbing my wanton mouth. Now, though, a silent, assertive licking between my thighs caused me to stir. Some old goat had slipped into my cabin and knelt quietly, lifting the skirt of my towel to sup at my divine cock.

My penis is neither tiny nor impressive. It is an adequate aqueduct of urine should my bowels process the occasional water I accidentally imbibe from the pools and showers. I reach orgasm only rarely, through the culmination of an intensely hot scene, when I have returned to a favorite bathhouse in Japan or Turkey, for instance. It is always hard for me *not* to cum at the Continental Baths in New York City. The glittering music there is maddeningly arousing, the men somehow different, their collective energy *the* zeitgeist of lust. Music! The silver bells of automated human hearts beat throughout the dance floor. Plus, the Continental is one of the few saunas with rooftop access, affording me a most infrequent view of that oceanic tapestry, the sky. I miss the stars, though the constellations are something of a painful reminder of my family tree. But the city. Oh, that city. New York City. Of course it is "new." It vanquishes Rome with its size, the teeming masses. From above I see that chariots have been automated, with glowing eyes and strange blares of lament whenever they gather in large numbers, which is often. A diadem of light seen from Olympus, no doubt.

So I work up from my sundry dreams and patted the top of the old goat lapping away between my legs, unsurprised to find the familiar dull nubs of worn horns. Zotikos. An actual satyr. We had crossed paths before. I had long known I was not the only mythological creature who haunted the baths. Though they were exceptionally rare, particularly when my travels took me forward in time, I found their occasional presence reassuring. Magic happens. Nothing was routine in the couplings of men. I had seen Zotikos throughout the eons, usually wintering in the warm confines of European bathhouses. No doubt, he summered outside, in sylvan plains. Wherever I discovered him, he was bounding about, his long, speckled brown and pink penis erupting from the goatish white hair that plaited his thighs and hind legs. Only I could tell he possessed a tail he had neatly trimmed into a nub, so he could traverse the human world without notice.

I shifted, and the old goat shot me a toothless grin and went back to work, the purplish knobs of his spine rolling with the ministrations of his mouth. I leaned back on my elbows and concentrated on the rare treat of pleasure given. The tongue that swabbed my tip might be gray but it was masterful, knowing, possessing a philosophical grip and a soulful surrender.

I intuited that the randy beast dutifully wished to swallow. The taste of my semen induces madness, however, blinding mortals and even the mythic with an ecstasy that melts their suspicious minds with its lightning sincerity. I had to deny him. I had only made the mistake of allowing a partner to sup from my rod once before, back in a Grecian bathhouse, when I was new to my travels and this divine aspect of my sex was unknown to me. My stricken patron was kept by the bathhouse in question, a fool on a golden chain staked to the floor in the middle of a low-ceilinged basement. Patrons fed him and cooed after this lost soul while they gently fucked him, for he was granted a certain amount of my allure. On occasion, I would find myself back there. My presence would always elicit a frenzy of orgiastic behavior from him—drooling, shitting, and animalistic groveling—reminding me that humans are, above all else, fragile.

With orgasm mounting, I gently pushed the satyr away with my blackened foot. The old goat was disappointed, but his mouth was still agape, hoping for a stray drop of semen. I wanted to both spare him madness and reward such a faithful servant. I stood above him, arching my back while working my member with lithe fingers. Head back and lips parted, with a swivel of my hips, I ejaculated a vigorous torrent of golden doves up into the air and when they plummeted back down caught the molten flock in my mouth.

I swallowed with a dramatic gulp, smiled, and did a slight curtsy. The old goat literally fell over and struggled to right himself, blinking, unbelieving but knowing. He offered rowdy applause and the slow, polite bow one master gives to another maybe once or twice in a lifetime.

CHAPTER FIVE

Surrender Complete

The sounds of Rome at night: the gallop of horses, the anxious and whispering feet of speeding messengers. The retching of drunks and the occasional, distant sob of an exhausted whore and her doorway paramour.

My brother's confident footsteps coming down the hall. I curled beneath my sheets into an even tighter ball, knowing he would mistake my position as that of ready plaything rather than fearful recoil. Until that night, I had thought his brusque brutality that of all boys entering manhood and about to don the *toga virillus,* not indicative of darker tastes. However, as we grew, I noticed more of our individual father's attributes emerging from within us. I could hold my breath in the bath for quite a long time. For Obsidio, the occasional black sparrow would drop dead from his unwavering gaze.

A bath previously drawn by Perseus, a hint of lavender in the cooling water to please me.

The bumpy ride home in the palanquin had been a journey toward terror. I was unsure if I had left him behind or if my brother would somehow beat me home. I thought briefly of telling our mother but then recalled that she was out, that Perseus was in charge of the household and, absent him, my lethal brother. I shook as I cried. Silent slaves let the palanquin down softly. They probably assumed my whimpering was over some immature love affair or a paltry comeuppance between me and my brother. They stood quietly at attention while I remained frozen among the pillows within what amounted to a silken casket, for I had been carried to my doom. Surely, Obsidio would silence me to keep me from telling Mother about his deadly secret. That's when I realized how valuable I was to him. Our shared maternal blood and immortal seed made me immune to his deadly semen. I was the only being on earth whose service he could enjoy more than once. I was the only one who knew how to please him. Everyone else was an inevitable victim, a roll of the dice in terms of whether he actually enjoyed the encounter, and if he did, it was never to be repeated. The guards opened the doors to our mansion, fortress-like in the torchlight. I entered, grimly aware of the role I must play.

❖

His footsteps came to a stop, but he did not enter my room.

I shivered to think he had moved on to additional prey in my absence. The entrance to the basement slave quarters was just down the hall.

Never once had I thanked Perseus for the lavender.

I let out a slight whimper, to tempt him, giving out the impression my sleep was troubled, that he could enter my dreams as easily as he could part my lips. If I could take enough of his seed, he would be too spent to visit others. I rolled and stretched in the bed as if stricken with nightmares, knowing my perceived terror would draw him in. The door opened. I could hear him circle my supine form. He pulled my sweat-soaked sheet away, and I gasped as he raked my chest with sharp nails. Pretending to be startled awake, I kicked against the mattress and ran my hands over my goose-fleshed skin, so sure was I his uncut nails had turned into ebony talons and that he had cut me, that I was bleeding.

"Not yet, little one," he whispered. "But I could make you bleed, if you'd like that."

The moonlight filtering through the window bounced off his slice of a smile. My room was Spartan, a few scrolls. In one corner a simple pedestal held an erotic amphora I had spied in the market one day and cried until Mother had purchased it for me, but not before she examined the gladiators entwined across its baked clay. With a finger, Obsidio tickled the bottom of my exposed feet.

"What's this? Sandy soles after a visit to the baths? Usually only your knees get dirty." He chortled drily. His laughter always had this slight echo, as if reverberating in an unseen cave, a low place of cruel rites and panicked sacrifice.

His toga dropped, and he arched his back, awaiting service. His body was icy marble in the darkness. An emerging tumescence beckoned. I flipped onto my stomach and swiveled to catch his cock in my mouth. Better to serve him than answer questions. I instinctively found his erection. Its stony hardness battered at my lips as I pretended to hesitate, to better provide him the mastery he craved. He sighed as I parted my lips and found his root with my tongue. He had not bathed since his visit to the Coliseum, and I tasted the sweat of other men, his own dried spore. And perhaps Perseus's last breath.

At that thought, I let out a brief cry, which he interpreted as the pain of submission and thrust deeper, harder. Movements made more to conquer than satisfy. I choked, tongue flat and eyes wide. Tears of vexation gathered at the corners of my eyes as I struggled against the onslaught. His thickness stretched my throat as I struggled to maintain some semblance of control, participation even. I meekly gripped his shaft to better assist his mounting orgasm, but he hissed the most serpentine noise and grabbed my wrists. Lissome hands pinned above my head, I relented. He leaned in to lick my tears. The bleak, utter coldness of his tongue, a genuine instrument of the underworld, burned my flesh. It was as if my face had brushed up against a dew-covered tombstone on a moonless winter's eve. Invisible spiders raced across my body at the very thought. My willpower dissipated, and I limited my efforts to simply sucking, to receiving his demanding penis and erasing any reminder of my corporeal being. All mouth, my surrender complete, he let go of my hands, and I clutched the back of his thighs to lock us together, the better to keep all of Rome safe. I had swallowed my pride, the pride of others, much salty semen, and the occasional lungful of pool water in my brief erotic life. Now I swallowed the darkness that could engulf so many others if I did not do a good enough job.

Mother would report Perseus as a runaway in the morning and have the rest of the household beaten, mostly in punishment for unspoken collusion in his escape, but also for a bit of sport.

CHAPTER SIX

Ocean of Lust

The line to enter the Baths of Caracalla was unusually long, and I was glad I had agreed to meet Publius beforehand. We were both excited and nervous, though Publius was able to relax a bit in his role of veteran, offering tidbits of advice. I wasn't sure if he was kidding or not when he told me to gargle with salt water and then suck on a lemon, a spectacular and expensive fruit recently introduced to Rome by eastern traders, so its potential medicinal powers were only now being discovered. I took his advice, meant to both massage my internal throat muscles and improve upon my pucker. I did both privately after a meager lunch, thinking even if it was a trick, it couldn't hurt. I kept lunch down to a few figs and some Parthian bread, as I wanted my bowels empty. Though fucking was forbidden at the event, I wanted to be prepared lest I was taken by surprise.

❖

The statue of a now-forgotten emperor loomed over the entrance like a disapproving tutor, admonishing his students for a lack of cleanliness. As this was the first time I had ever had to wait to gain entrée, I pondered the statue. The hands and head had been replaced. The faint necklace of a scar encircled the throat, barely concealed by peeling paint. An army of repurposed statues occupied Rome. When the rabble turns on an emperor, statues are pulled down during the ensuing riots. Less sturdy models lose a nose, and hands often break at the wrist. With order returned, typically after a desultory round of executions and perfunctory donations to the Praetorian Guard, with the senate having passed grandiose proclamations in support of whoever snatched the bloodied purple, said statues were rarely righted. For when the populace of Rome turns against its ruler, there is no going back. For example, I had never seen the likeness of Nero or Commodus. I was fascinated by both, as they were rumored to have the same predilections I had. What most considered egregious slander caused me to read every bit of gossip I could about their ruinous reigns. During his rule, Nero publicly married another man. I've not been able to locate the infamous panegyrics detailing the ceremony, though I have read that several prominent *pathicus* imitated the ritual to curry imperial favor, as did many others regardless of their actual preferences. The body of the statue above had most likely belonged to Caracalla, the fratricidal emperor assassinated while taking a piss along a dirt road in Turkey. His only lasting contribution to the empire, as far as I knew, was the construction of this beautiful bath, one of the architectural jewels of a city filled with bathhouses, public and private. Or so I was told in the *caldarium* one afternoon. We Romans love to cleanse ourselves while submitting to the dirtiest gossip imaginable. Though imported from ancient Greece, we improved and expanded upon the concept of the bathhouse to such a degree that we easily surpassed those modest civic efforts. Our public bathhouses could hold several thousand people, though the wealthiest had private baths installed in their homes. Our mansion in the city was old and the neighborhood built up, so thankfully this was not possible for our household. However, I was deeply disappointed that our villa in Baiae was expansive and modern, meaning it possessed the most luxurious bathing facilities available, placing the rumored profligate local bathhouse forever out of my reach.

Once, when I was shopping with Mother for a statue to adorn the new fountain she was planning for the portico, I had caught her wrinkling her nose at an adorable Cupid the merchant had shown us. The shop contained a dusty army of philosophers and Olympians, as well as half-finished tombstones awaiting payment on the next installment, past due. In the confines of our curtained palanquin, I asked her why she had passed on what I thought was a delightful, spritely figure.

"Because that was a statue of a very young Caligula, dear. Back when he was called Little Boots and adored by the army. After his assassination, his statues were tossed to the ground, but some enterprising artisan must have hauled one into his workshop, glued some wings to his back, and sanded off that infamous smirk. It's been passed around as an antique ever since." As the slaves hoisted us up, she smiled with a sense of self-satisfaction that would have rivaled anything that ever crossed Caligula's face.

"And besides, we don't want him in our delightful garden. What does a dictator know about love?"

I looked at my mother in a rare moment of admiration.

Caligula. However, now our garden was trammeled by something much darker than a mere mercurial, moody, and very mortal emperor.

❖

Publius and I made our way to the entrance beneath the shadow of the decapitated dictator. I thought again of Obsidio. I had been hesitant to leave him home alone and had barely stepped foot outside our house since that night at the Coliseum. I was as servile as possible toward my brother, and this morning had woken my dark sibling by taking his hard cock in my mouth while he was still asleep. He had barely acknowledged my service between his spread legs, grunting in his sleep as his satisfaction issued forth. Once again, after our morning exercises with the tutor, I studiously drained him in the library while he rested a scroll atop my head. I paid special attention to the glans, enough so that I felt him shift in appreciation as I gulped down a prodigious amount of seed. I visited his room after our Greek lessons, pretending interest in his sparse collection of scrolls until he noticed me and wordlessly beckoned me onto the bed with an impertinent nod of his head. There I played with his feet and toes and then licked his thighs. Working my way up, by the time I made it to his tunic, his penis had tentatively extended, like some hibernating animal seeking sustenance. I again took it in my mouth. While I sucked and teethed I prayed that, suitably depleted, he would drift off to sleep and that it would be safe for me to again leave him alone for the night.

CHAPTER SEVEN

The Threats of Desire

Having arrived at the baths, the challenge to remain chaste until the Fellatiolympics was good cause to explore the reason I had started coming there in the first place, the public library. An amazing amount of knowledge was arrayed within these marbled halls. History, philosophy, poetry—so much was contained in the baths that, along with the shops and food stalls that connected the libraries, one could spend all day here luxuriating in the various pools hot and cold, with new ideas in reach and wine and food just around the corner. However, we were not interested in corners. Our next adventure was beneath the baths, hidden in basement chambers supporting the furnaces that made the heated waters of the *caldarium* possible. At first, time moved slowly. No scroll I pulled from the shelf could hold my attention. I tried not to study the men and guess who was here to take in a good soak and who was here to participate in the evening's ceremonies. I spied foreign men who I had not previously seen at the baths but tried not to let my eyes linger on their equipment, in an attempt to store my erotic energy for what was to come.

As the afternoon waned, I lost sight of Publius and grew concerned that he would think I had lost my nerve. I strolled around, hoping I was as conspicuous as possible so my friend would easily spot me. The baths were crowded as usual. The clamor of conversation reached a near roar around the more populated pools. I wanted to linger every time my eye caught a glimpse of a floating penis of interesting girth or length, but I needed to keep moving. In our excited chatter about the event, I had never bothered to ask exactly how I would gain entry, so I was relying on Publius. If *he* had lost nerve and left, all was lost. I slowly circled the outdoor pool. The shimmering mosaic at the bottom of the pool illustrated Pompey the Great's victory over a pirate fleet. The tiled images of sea monsters gathered beneath the dangling feet of resting swimmers. Dejected, I thought to take one last plunge before heading home. Suddenly Publius put a hand on my shoulder. Relieved, I smiled. He motioned with his eyes for me to look up. The sky had darkened and attendants were lighting torches. I knew that certain columns concealed doorways that the bathhouse attendants used to access the areas below the facilities. A discreet stream of men and boys slipped behind the blue shadows of the columns. Publius took my hand and we followed. The games had begun.

The Fellatiolympics. Rich, ecclesiastical incense clung to the ceiling of the winding corridor, curving around the brick, rounding it out until I felt as if we were being ushered down into a cave where a sibyl would speak of our futures. Beneath the main furnaces of the *hypocaust*, the massive heating system, lay a warren of tunnels as well as a large ancillary room where the Fellatiolympics was hosted every Lupercalia. A tall, thin eunuch with an appropriately droopy, bulbous nose knowingly divined who was here to serve and who was to be serviced, silently separating the herd of men with nothing more than a raised eyebrow beneath a phallus-shaped headpiece. His own clipped testicles, tanned into leather pouches and filled with magical spices, hung so low from his wizened ears that they grazed his shoulders.

We huddled with our fellow catamites. Everyone snuck looks at one another while whispering with comrades. Some of the more experienced participants stretched and limbered up like athletes before a javelin throw, or some such wholesome and banal contest. *Well, it is a competition*, I thought. Self-consciously, I began to mimic some of the neck exercises until Publius snorted, and I stopped. The eunuch briskly ushered everyone into line, and a drunk, red-faced man I recognized as the bath's resident physician, followed by a slave hoisting a lamp, began examining us one by one. We all expectantly opened our mouths and stuck out our tongues as he peered inside, searching for cankers or disqualifying discoloration. He uttered a dismissive "tsk, tsk" as one diminutive prostitute resisted opening his mouth. The eunuch pried open the boy's ruddy lips with the end of a phallus-tipped rod. The boy rolled his eyes and dropped his jaw. The physician sniffed the boy's breath and peered inside. He shook his head and moved to the next catamite as the eunuch clucked his tongue and ushered the boy-prostitute down the smoky hallway. After the inspection, a somber young priest poured everyone a mouthful of strong wine with an aftertaste of unknown herb. I dutifully swallowed and looked to Publius for support, but his thoughts were on the coming games, mouth open in anticipation.

The eunuch had finished inspecting us and was now arranging the men opposite by size. Some protested and insisted on a higher order. There stood the infamous gladiators Placidus, who was anything but, and Wido, a tribal warrior captured in the Black Forest of Germania. Ironically, the forest that sprung from his abdomen was the darkest I had ever seen, made more so as the long serpent that swung from within this unruly wreath was of such a pristine alabaster that its internal veins glowed an unearthly blue. Both enjoyed their position at the front of the line. They stretched and squatted in unison, flexing their thick, sword-and-trident scarred thigh muscles while pivoting their hips to better display massive, dangling cocks. To prepare for the games, they had oiled their bodies. Placidus's form was almost completely depilated. The gladiators shone like Apollo's stallions beneath the subterranean moons of torchlight.

The strength of the herb concealed with the wine began to make itself felt. Steam undulated like luminescent seaweed beneath an ocean of lust. Meaning I was in my element. My vision darkened on the edges, my view of the room narrowed, and the men I was meant to serve came into greater focus. Defined chests and muscled stomachs or smooth scholars, effete slaves with renowned members, the kinds of pythonic cocks that inspire latrine poetics; short, tall, skinny, young, old; gladiators, senators, merchants, soldiers, dirty poets and crazy novelists, mad philosophers, and sunburned foreigners who had crossed violent seas just to participate. All here for the Fellatiolympics, a secret, sacred contest. The God Priapus was in this very room, commanding me and my fellow catamites to ride every cock presented to us with our talented tongues and knowing throats. I homed in on the meat meant for my mouth. I was not going to fall off. I was going to win. I deserved every pearl.

Publius, in his excitement, had failed to brief me on the various competitions. I had lost him the minute the priests summoned us to action. I did not care. I did not need him now that we were competitors. Somewhere in the pit of my stomach was a thirst like a whirlpool, black waters overwhelming frail little me, and I was more than willing to be caught and drowned by the threats of desire.

For the first event, we were commanded with elaborate,

ancient hand gestures to kneel on individual worn marble wheels. My knees were tied down with thick leather straps as my hands were secured behind my back. Blindfolded, I was discombobulated as the wheel began to spin. I could not discern my role, as, picking up speed, a variety of cocks began to poke and prod at my face, slapping my cheeks, pushing up against one nostril or the other. Blind, in the darkest depths, all I knew was my sharpening need. I strained to catch a cock, latch on to any member, draw anything into my mouth and properly nurse it to its plumpest, most perfect state, until it populated my throat. And in striving to do so, I realized the rules of the game. *Desperation would unseat me.* If I fell, I lost the competition. Moderation was the aim here, to tease, not to please. These sexual warriors needed to fulfill their purpose throughout the night, and I, myself, was meant to last. Therefore, I imagined I was a dandelion licking the wind. And with that, the wind licked back. As the stone wheel picked up speed, this thickening, hardening pinwheel of penises began to slash my cheeks. Expertly, I stuck out my tongue and intuited shape and need. Thus, I was able to tantalize the assailing cocks, pleasing these hidden men to the extent that several members started awarding my tongue with those slow, initial convulsions of semen that lubricated the best of nights.

The next contests consisted of servicing standing and then sitting men. We were given a moment's reprieve while we rinsed our mouths with watered-down wine. A trembling ephebe vomited up a torrent of moist morsels and several sad suckers leapt to lap up the milky porridge, to prove they were the most intemperate, as if additional medals were given for debauched hunger. We were then directed to squat before a line of centurions, senators, gladiators, and even some favored slaves, equal in their monstrous girth. Behind them, another phalanx stood ready. Diminutive slaves, plucked and primped, suckled and licked at their impressive lengths in preparation.

My lips felt bruised. I swallowed. This night would try my strength, my soul, and definitely my lower jaw. My bare feet pressed into the smooth, slippery stone. The heat of the room rose, the sexual energy, the expectant breath, steam from the roiling furnaces, all gathered to form a cloud that clung like ghostly moss to the ceiling. My exposed and spread ass actually felt slightly chilly as the workings of the bathhouse above pulled all of the heat upward. The eunuch-priest made an elaborate, mystical motion, lit some incense, and we all placed our hands behind our backs as glans met tongue. The man I serviced smiled down at me, and that encouragement gave me everything I needed to make the extra effort; my mouth stretched near the breaking point. His thickness was that of a small arm, an arm that hoisted a palanquin, rowed a slave ship, so honed and veiny, pulsing, as if he were excreting muscle down my throat. I knew to relax and let him drive. Obsidio had taught me well; I bought time by paying slavish attention to the head, nursing the salty slit, edging my tongue inside as much as possible to halt his plunder and prepare for the inevitable length storming my throat. He grunted, I relented, and downward he dove. Filled, pummeled, I surrendered. My knees slipped on the floor beneath his unrelenting pressure. Past surrender, I imagined my body was an extension of his, the reverse of a serpent shedding its skin. He was pulling me on like a tight girdle, and I needed to empty myself, abandon any sense of my separateness, really. When I did, he was able to enter me more fully, and I steadied myself against his sweaty thighs. His rolling testicles separated to press against either of my cheeks, while my stretched lips were smeared with saliva and the slick ooze of semen, providing further adhesion. Out of the corner of my tearful eye, I could see the competition was, in equal measure, also nearly knocked senseless. Publius was close. The beast riding his face was none other than the gladiator Wido. Two priapic priests stood nearby in case he swooned, and, in fact, as the German bucked wildly, the boy's bowels loosed and slender brown fingers of shit plopped out. Prepared for this eventuality, one of the priests calmly motioned for a slave, equipped with a small broom and dustpan, to collect the droppings. Though Publius never once let the cock slip out of his mouth and continued with renewed vigor, the watchful priests each raised an eyebrow toward the other. His score had been lowered. My Minotaur unloaded without warning, and I dutifully swallowed, extending my arms as if a bird in flight, in mimicry of the Phoenix, his voluminous cum the molten lava from which the fiery bird was birthed. Some in the waiting and watching crowd noticed this artistic flourish, which elicited no small amount of soft, appreciative applause.

❖

A number of participants passed out. A few wept from exhaustion and begged to be excused, but most of us were crafty soldiers long at war with our own lust and ready for unrelenting battle. The incense grew thicker, and it was harder to see. Not that we needed to. Blindfolded again, my fellow catamites and I were next led into a steam room where various participants lined the marble benches carved into the ornate walls. We were pushed to our knees and ordered to crawl toward our momentary masters. Asses up, feet crushed fingers, a few elbows nudged ribs, all quietly, as no one wanted points deducted. My hands found a pair of feet, hoary toenails and thick ankles. I dove in with my mouth and found a limp but weighty penis. Its massive form twitched at first and then slowly expanded as I gave it an initial lick and then nestled its rough head against my warm cheek. I gripped the owner's thick calves as he grunted and spread his legs to accommodate my lithe form. I curled within the heat of his lap as his length wormed its way down my throat; his musk was of the darkest depths of the sea, a rich black salt of exertion and the taste of dried ambrosia, much like the mineral undercurrent of Obsidio's spunk. I swooned but righted myself, blinking beneath the blindfold.

Either his cock is magical, or this man is a god. Or cursed. What if his cock was cursed by some witch, and all my teeth will fall out? Or my tongue turns black? Or becomes forked, like that of an adder?

I swallowed my panic and the last of the Minotaur's semen that had been sticking to the roof of my mouth and went back to work. His pubic mass was the thickest I had ever encountered in my young life. It scraped against my brow like heavy palm fronds. Copious foreskin undulated within my mouth. The head further engorged, suppressing my tongue. It was a complex muscle, ridged beneath the foreskin, almost like gills. My efforts at ministrations had loosed the blindfold. I couldn't see his face. It was obscured by a large, hard belly, as scarred as a legionnaire's shield. The tip of his gnarled beard swung low like heavy moss. His length expanded my throat, demanding full attention. However, before I could again focus on gulping down more of his hard girth, a sharp pucker of purple glinted off his stomach. I squinted.

Is that a barnacle?

I gagged, and he grunted displeasure as the blindfold fell away and I pulled back. The unruly hair clogging my nostrils rolled like seaweed at high tide. I steadied myself by gripping his feet and discovered webbed toes. Like mine were sometimes, if I lingered too long in the bath or the deep end of the pool.

I let his cock fall from out my mouth.

"Fa-fa-father?"

When did I see him last? When he swaddled me within the strength of one arm while Mother cooed over me. I remembered his smell: night tide, the sweat of drowning men.

And now I knew his taste.

"Nerites!"

Neptune. He violently kicked me away from his saliva-drenched crotch. I skidded across the slick floor and actually turned circles, knocking into the other contestants who strenuously pushed me back toward the middle of the room, their expert servicing mostly uninterrupted.

"You. Nerites, you are the lowest of the low."

Neptune. Lightning flickered at the corner of his eyes. I tried to hurry away, but the floor was so slick with semen, saliva and condensation from the steam that I wheeled about in place, terrified.

"You are nothing more than a sea roach, scurrying about at the feet of filthy mortals."

His teeth sharpened and multiplied into those of a shark.

"How dare you debase *our* holy ichor."

This echoed throughout the chamber, and though nothing could shake this fraternity of cocksuckers from their servitude, the men before them looked at one another wildly, trapped and fearful.

Eyeless, wheezing emerald eels parted the white sea foam of Neptune's interwoven beard and hair. Their black maws revealed needle-like fangs. He shook his head in utter disgust.

"You want to sup on mortal members, little sea fairy?

Well, so be it. Why don't you spend eternity on your knees, licking the meek tridents of measly men? In fact, let it be as essential to you as the air they breathe!"

Lightning crackled from out his eyes as he extended an Olympic fist within which his trident magically appeared. He pounded the end onto the marble floor, which cracked. My fellow suckers finally slowed as their partners all lifted their feet and tried to somehow retreat into the wet walls behind them. Ocean water flowed up through the newly formed fissure, ushering in luminescent white crabs and twisting, furious blue sea snakes while the central darkness of this emerging tide pulled me forward. My last sight was father, his attention already turned away from the disappointment of my petty being and toward a cowering, effeminate boy stuck between the legs of the unconscious gladiator Wido, who, overcome by the sight of an angry god, had passed out.

As Neptune beckoned the little slave to finish what I had started, water washed over my head, and the eddy that would swallow me time and time again gripped my body and my mind as a familiar thirst, one that had defined my short life up until that point, guttered within me into a permanent, spiritual drought. One that I would forever work and fail to quench.

CHAPTER EIGHT

Night and Snow

The water churned as I surfaced, and I gasped and blinked and the tiled mural of samurai came into focus. Some of the warriors stood naked and aroused, some were about to disrobe, taken by surprise by an enemy army while bathing in a river. Kimonos neatly part so the viewer may study the pink swords of their erections. The vast battle scene covers an entire wall, as intricate as it is simple. The rippling folds of withdrawn foreskin revealed the proud and martial helmets of flesh, as red as the carp nipping at submerged heels. How I relished these excursions onto Japanese soil. As far as I could tell, the most sexually civilized population on earth, an island nation truly apart in terms of refinement and beauty. This magnificent country was not known to the Roman Empire during my youth, but I can only imagine what foes or allies they would have made. I savor Japanese men, the quiet wolf of their masculinity untamed by unnatural religions or desultory cultural demands. Their bathhouses are always meticulously clean. Simple oases of austere communal bathing, places offering respite as well as sexual release, the Japanese sauna has been one of the few places that remind me of the Roman baths because they often have intimate reading rooms neatly lined with books. These compacted versions of scrolls are still undecipherable to me, though the illustrated texts are pure marvels of carnality. Whenever I arrive in Japan, my stomach growls in anticipation of not only the wholesome sperm I would gulp down but the delicious neon sodas, the skewers skinny golden boys roast over charcoal-filled braziers, red knees separating white towels as they lean close to sear meat over flame. These dark dens of fucking, feasting, and napping, how I loved the little waves of snoring and sighing that rose from the matted sleep chambers as their occupants rested between bouts of sodomy.

I emerged from the tub, and astonished men stared, then looked at one another for confirmation. An old man squatting on a small plastic stool, vigorously scrubbed himself. At his gnarled feet, a handheld showerhead dribbled warm water. He looked up at me and smiled. He remembered me from decades ago when he was young, when Osaka had more wooden houses than concrete apartment complexes. He was not at all perplexed that I had not aged. He gave a slight nod as I passed. I patted his head lightly and paused, trying to remember the way to the sauna. Maybe he thought I was a lost and horny river kappa. No, his smile deepened after our brief interlude. The erotic is eternal. To touch is to forget your age or inexperience and simply commune. He giggled and rose, thinking to capture me again within the folds of the steam, salt my mouth and therefore link again with his younger self, a wormy our ouroboros of timeless semen. I nodded in affirmation but wished for a stroll before taking his now pert penis between my eager lips. He settled again into his ritual of washing, a physical meditation, really. One I was happy to partake in soon, for I had planned to settle into this bathhouse haven for as long as possible.

❖

Kappa. A perennial pest in the otherwise aquatic paradise of Japanese saunas. These green duck-billed goblins are some of the only relics from the country's mythic past. Most creatures were content to fade into other realms as freeways unfurled and high rises rose, but not the persistently obstinate kappa; they simply adjusted, relocating to sewers and saunas. When a young, buff man ignores the insistent attentions of what he dismissively considers a troll, he is sometimes closer to the truth then he could imagine. However, to be rude to a kappa invites reproach. Towels go stolen, wallets disappear, shoes are suddenly a size too small. Some of the older sauna employees are wise to their mischief and discreetly place cucumbers, the kappa's preferred food, behind the used towel bins in an appreciated act of appeasement. When that is done with regularity, socks rarely go missing and keys are never lost.

❖

The tub wooden, water a perfect temperature, I soaked and splashed around alone, luxuriating in the knowledge that I would stay here for a while. It must have been late at night, though. The bathhouse was quiet. No one had entered the vestibule where shoes were removed and coins deposited. Dim rooms with bunk beds stacked with sleeping men. As always, the sauna and tubs were fastidious and sparkling. A thin young man entered, naked save for a small hand towel he held discreetly before his bulging genitals. Tufts of the blackest hair, like a shock of pine needles, poked out in every direction from around the clutched cloth. He froze when he realized he was not alone, and he hesitated before continuing into the steam room. I remembered this sauna from previous visits and knew he had just emerged from a warren of small rooms within the basement; you needed a secret password to enter as it was meant for men under the age of thirty. I had gained entry on every visit, me, the oldest being to ever grace the premises, excusing the kappa, who likely do not age. I certainly do not age. I just swim through time.

Time and water.

Water and time.

Really, measuring both qualities is such a worthless endeavor. After all, they do just *flow*. They both flow through your fingers as easily and frequently as they move through the unhinged jaws of disintegrating skulls at the bottom of various seas. Still, I have had the urge to test the limits of my confining-yet-oh-so-exploratory journey. I cannot step outside a bathhouse or I will be summarily whipped back into the deep end of the dirtiest pool in some other era, mostly unaffected, save a sore neck. However, I can enjoy "nature" so long as I am still within the confines of bathhouse property. Meaning I have sunned myself in garden grottos and stood on rooftops to see blinking stars through tearful eyes. Establishments with such trappings are rare, as the very purpose of these institutions is to be hidden, internal, insular. Here, however, I knew the stairs led up to an outdoor smoking patio affording a banal view of other buildings and an anemic slice of sky, but it was here I first saw snow. Night and snow. The surprise of the cold. Mater Roma never felt like this in the most bracing of my childhood winters, yet it was a delicious difference.

The closest I had ever gotten to seeing snow was ice brought down from the Alps for a banquet. I remember the evening well, as it was the month of August and Mother, who rarely entertained, invited an unusual assortment of guests to our villa in Baiae. I was allowed to stay up to witness the spectacle of ice. Slaves brought it into the dining room upon a silver platter, their entire bodies painted white. They had been instructed to exaggeratedly shiver and hold each other for warmth once the ice had been deposited in the center of the low table covered with a smattering of dishes containing half-eaten delicacies. Divans with lounging guests surrounded the scene. Soon the slaves began to show signs of arousal and the guests applauded and began to take off their clothes, as this signaled that the feast had officially transitioned to an orgy. I was ushered out, but not before I touched the ice, already perspiring as drunken senatorial wives raced around the room. But I didn't get to taste it. Here on this island nation, it occasionally snows. The night sky is a dark canvas of floating white petals that melt upon my hot tongue.

I love Japan.

❖

A warren of sighs and gray shadows, of thoughtful figures in repose surrounded a grunting pair, one restrained by others as an earnest boy worked a fist deep inside the other's forgiving rose. I forever marvel at the self-discipline of the genuine voyeur, something unique to this culture. In Europe and the Americas, men who happen upon other men having sex in saunas either join in or observe. In watching, they regress into a hunched pack of masturbatory jackals. Not the Japanese. The Japanese watch as if taking in some private sport, divining new techniques, appraising the skill of others. The fist in a dark room. Raw contact to fill more than an opening, pummel the void and, what, exchange pleasure for pain?

Viewing this act opened up my own full flower of thirst. I dropped to my knees, and a group of men, naked or wearing open, short kimonos of stiff cloth converged. I parted my lips and extended my tongue, awaiting their offers. A fat dick head rubbed across my nose, and I leaned in to catch it. Some of the men waved their cocks in my face, teasingly, thumbs on stiff shafts protruding from shredded nets of pubic hair. Others hit my eyelids with cummy cockheads or prodded my cheeks. Dizzy, I tried to touch them all with my tongue, eyes closed, silently begging them to lead me from the dark and into the light. Semen splashed across my eyes, and I sucked a man who, instead of shooting in my mouth, painted my lips white. The baptismal ritual of *bukkake* had commenced. Men pulled on their dicks as I sat supplicant still, awaiting anointment. The light applause of multiple men whipping their cocks wafted throughout the chamber. Some would dip their penises into my mouth for momentary lubrication. Others circled, touching no one but themselves, pulling out their orgasms like rare albino birds coaxed toward initial flight. Others fucked my face. The old man from my earlier visits observed this sexual parlance from the shadows as if watching a familiar ritual, sorting for new rites, awaiting the appropriate opportunity to anoint my lips. Some of the men laid their cocks across either shoulder and waited patiently until I could take them up and into my mouth. All doused my head until my skull was laced with drizzled white loops of primordial ooze.

The chorus of masturbation faded as each man finished on my face and stepped away toward the showers. The air cooled as less animalistic friction heated the confined space. I felt a kind, coarse hand pet my head in the darkness and knew it was him. He had mounted my face vigorously all those years ago, and after he had come in my mouth, he took me into one of the small sleeping rooms, laid me down without a word, and held me as we both slept on a thin tatami mat.

Here, he parted my sticky, swollen lips with a slice of his finger, to clear a path for his throbbing penis. I nibbled at the head, just as I had done those decades past, and he whispered sweetly in Japanese. I could smell the whiskey and cigarettes on his breath. His cock tasted of nicotine from his masturbatory efforts. His familiar thrusts were more deliberate, practiced. I moved my tongue in unison and let out an alluring cry. He linked his fingers behind my skull to better control my reciprocity. Jaw lowered, head tilted, I teethed on his length in my mouth but sensed he was pausing, measuring his movements. He wanted this to last, this reclamation of his youth. I slowed my sucking to match his rhythm. His buttocks trembled as he tried to withhold orgasm, but I pushed myself forward until I had the hairy root of his penis firmly within my mouth and he relented. I swallowed as he exhaled. We disengaged. I felt his presence as he regarded me for a while, this sodden, eternal ghost. Like the others, he departed for a shower or a soak in one of the tubs. If he stayed the night, I would find him. For now I was complacent just sitting still, eyes sealed shut, happy to be rooted in one spot for a change. Wishing the strands that dripped from my chin and ear would actually take root in the ground, grow and solidify, until I was unmoving, not a statue but a fountain that flowed in reverse, fed by all of the men in Japan.

Darkness and white petals that melt upon my hot tongue.

How I love Japan.

CHAPTER NINE

Comes the Ocean

Subterranean swimming pools cast an aquamarine hue across beveled ceilings ensconced with plaster cherubs who intermittently deposit flakes of white excreta into the serene waters below. I can float on my back for hours or somersault over and over in such environs. The sound of my fabricated waves licking the tiles echoes throughout the chamber. I love a good plunge. However, this is a rarity. By their very design and economy of space, the majority of bathhouses do not possess pools of note.

Those that do provide me a distinct oasis, one where I tend to linger and luxuriate, leisurely swimming to exercise away the charley horses that come from hours of servile squatting. Certainly some of the finer, larger establishments have outdoor or even rooftop pools. These I enjoy, especially if I have gone a long time without exposure to the sun's poetic rays, piercing or caressing my naked body depending on the season. But I prefer the underground pools, the way the light ripples across dark and dimpled ceilings. These black wombs feel like my intended home, or rather the epicenter of this startling rebirth. I emerge from these cerulean waters the rarest animal in the world, naked and dripping, ready to feed solely on lust. These are my underwater kingdoms, and if my aquatic roads and watery bridges occasionally lead to these manmade lakes, so be it. Such discoveries are a welcome respite before the next frolic, making the awaiting human banquet taste that much more succulent.

Traipsing through these linked labyrinths, pathways of ecstasy interrupted by cool, refreshing plunges and then dark dungeons, I encounter desert pockets as well. Whether it's the result of an off-season, an ungodly hour, or bad reputation, I occasionally happen upon an empty sauna. Even worse is finding myself alone in a basement maze. This can be disconcerting, to the say the least. Empty spaces devoid of both humanity and the water I require for transport. When this happens, I try not to let panic overtake me, for I usually need only retrace my steps, though sometimes this is difficult, for these warrens, designed to create as many corners and dead ends as possible to increase the probability of erotic encounters, can lead to confusion when the goal is to escape, not mate.

Alone, I find the air in these dead zones stale, cold, slightly bubonic, the uneven walls slicked with a mucus-like slime, odd corners populated by cummy fauna, miniature emerald patches of fuzz punctuated by tiny black mushrooms. I have stalked many a barren hall of crumbling brick fortified by shadow and the stench of stale urine. These low-ceilinged tunnels, unpopulated save for the scurry of an unseen rat or that eerily distant drip of water, that alluring sustenance of my travels, always makes me miss the ocean.

I miss the ocean.

You would think that with my lineage, I would know more about the sea, be more *of* the sea, which I do take after, in my own web-toed fashion. Tricks tell me that when I giggle, I sound like a twee little porpoise. When I was a young boy and Rome was stifling hot in high summer, my family habitually retreated to our seaside villa in Baiae. Though my mother abhorred the sun, she did enjoy proximity to the imperial family, which historically summered there as well. My older brother and I were only ever at the shore in the company of slaves and the children of the other vacationing upper class, quietly competing to display their wealth—publicly by erecting elaborate tents on the sand, privately by procuring the most gorgeous slaves imaginable to satisfy their sexual desires, lending them to friends and neighbors as well, for Baiae had a well-deserved reputation for licentiousness.

At the beach, I was happy to play with the other children, though my brother's darker bent was already showing as he shunned the sun, roughhousing with boys his own age, and he certainly ignored me so artfully his actions were almost admirable in their consistency and complexity. He almost never acknowledged my presence unless forced to do so by social convention. He constantly positioned our attendants to obscure his view of me.

I was fine amusing myself, however. On the beaches of Baiae, before it got too hot, I would collect all manner of shells and combine them into intricate piles, shaping with my small hands moats and walls and little rooms, all to be filled by the incoming tides. Looking back now, was I somehow prescient of my current fate? Was I, in fact, accidental architect to the mazes I currently inhabit?

Surely my mother first encountered my father at one of these seaside excursions. (Midnight swim, the aphrodisiac of menstruation.) Before I was born, she had entered a marriage of convenience with a rich senator who needed access to her even greater fortune from a previous marriage. Additionally, this arrangement concealed for them both sexual proclivities best exercised far from the marriage bed. They tactically divorced once he achieved the desired proconsulship and their fortunes had increased to the point where the public leverage she provided was no longer necessary. Marriage had allowed her to carry on no small amount of affairs with married men, but as a divorcée, she was always suspect and vulnerable to an onslaught of suitors. Though I was born while she was married, I was too young to remember her husband and too self-conscious of my divine lineage to ever mistake him for my father. This senator did not sire my brother, either. He and I look nothing alike, as we have different fathers whose sole similarity is their shared immortality. He was born during her first marriage, the source of her current wealth. As proximity to the ocean introduced Mother to my progenitor, closeness to death delivered her the eternal paramour whose dark seed begat my yet darker kin. Her first husband was a rich merchant who had died of the pox.

One terrible summer, most of Rome had emptied out as deadly plague swept over the city like a fire through a parched forest. I only know of this story having heard one of the older slaves whisper it to one newly purchased from Hispania. One of the younger slave girls showed the fever and the dark swellings beneath both armpits that heralded the plague. The other slaves were terrified and abandoned her in the basement quarters. The household, like much of the city, was in an uproar. The roads were choked with carts and palanquins making their escape. The bodies of beggars curled within the doorways of shuttered shops exuded a haze of black flies and putrid odor. At night, the Campania Mars glowed red with deep fire pits filled with the dead and, it was rumored, the forsaken doomed and still dying.

Mother ordered the household slaves to pack essentials and, under the command of Perseus, to flee the city and prepare the Baiae villa for her and her husband's eventual arrival. She alone would wait for his return, for he was in

Ostia, just outside of Rome. As a wealthy merchant, he had rushed to the port town to ensure his warehouses were secure, for such calamity often invited pirates. Mother kept only one slave behind, a mute but reliable oaf deeply devoted to her. Her stated and noble goal was to await her husband, but the story this slave had grimly pantomimed for his compatriots was quite the opposite.

When her husband returned after battling the crowds along the Appian Way, he was drained by the roadside carnage he had witnessed. Entire families had been wiped out by the plague, carts with all their possessions overturned and looted while carrion birds wove greedy patterns overhead. She served him a Spartan dinner and strong wine. It is likely they both perfunctorily cursed whichever out-of-favor sect the emperor had blamed for the pestilence, As these outbreaks crop up every few years, I have often heard Mother repeat the well-turned phrase "plagues give a carpenter calluses," for these workmen serve double duty, carving out coffins for the dead while erecting crucifixes for that season's screaming zealots.

Whatever draught she added to her husband's wine guaranteed a sound sleep. When he awoke in their darkened chambers, he rolled over to embrace her still form and recoiled. The cold body beside him was that of the now-dead slave girl. Her skin molted, crepuscular. He jumped out of bed and rushed to the door, only to find it bolted from the other side. He pounded and pleaded while Mother went about her household duties, making sure that whatever provisions the slaves did not take with them were not perishable, for she did not know how long they would be at the villa in Baiae.

The only sure timetable was that she would not leave the house until her husband had not only been stricken by the plague but had extinguished from it. He shouted, he begged, he demanded and then, much later, he whispered memories of their courtship. He apologized profusely for forgotten anniversaries and slights unknowingly delivered over the years. She busied herself by packing essential papers and determining what of her remaining wardrobe was suitable travel wear during such troubling times. She only ever smiled when she heard the telltale cough issue from their bedroom. Her slave spent all of his time in his quarters, terrified, copiously weeping. He had long ago had his tongue cut out, to better prepare him for servitude.

The stench of the dead slave girl permeated the house, as did the fumes of burning incense meant to mask the offensive odor. Mother's grim vigil continued as she then had to wait the appropriate amount of time it would take for her husband to either perish from the plague or, in his weakened state, starve to death. The slave knew exactly when his master expired, for that corresponded with the arrival of Pluto.

Her husband coughed hollowly from behind the door and fell silent. It was a dark, moonless night. The air was still as a figure emerged from out of the shadows of the atrium. Pluto was not the haggard ironsmith nor the beast of fire as depicted in so many murals and paintings. He walked into the dining room casually, like a man of means, his toga black and his skin midnight as well. He so exuded darkness, it was hard to make out his features other than his black hair, black eyes, and black lips. With each step he took toward Mother, he snapped his black fingers, and with each snap a candle was snuffed out, then an oil lamp. Once all the lights were out, he took her in his dark arms, raised his hand, and opened his moist palm to the night. With a final snap, the quivering mute slave went blind.

❖

When Mother finally arrived at the villa, the household slaves had already begun to take small liberties, sneaking sips of the best wine and the like, assuming that all who remained behind in Rome had perished. She was so willing to fully commit to the role of distracted, mournful widower that she punished no one. Everyone in Baiae had an opportunity to see her in her black toga. Few noticed the brooch, a simple silver key. It would have easily been mistaken as a token of affection, a present from the departed. But the symbol of the key was as dear to Pluto as the trident was important to his brother, Neptune.

She had long told family, friends, and acquaintances the tale of her brave husband tending to the sick girl, disregarding the risk to himself, and how both had eventually expired of the pestilence. She did not mention that upon arriving in Baiae, exhausted from the trying journey, she first stopped at her attorney's home. There she delivered a fresh copy of her husband's will before traveling on to her own estate, locally renowned for its inviting view of the ocean.

Obsidio was born approximately ten months later. It was a long, assiduously difficult pregnancy and then birth. He clung to Mother's womb, he so loved the darkness.

❖

Had I known how rare the sea would be to me in later life, I would have drunk in those early days, lingered on the shore more, rushing back in for another swim as the slaves dried our laundry on the rocks. As immensely satisfying as my life is now, I miss the ocean, though I still have a very personal connection with it, for now the sea rises from within me, after a particularly raucous bacchanalia, where I have served multitudes and been used repeatedly until the point of engorgement. Then comes the ocean, slow and sure, an internal tide that issues forth in driblets from between my bruised lips. Regurgitated white honey tapped from countless, breathless men.

Primal salt from the sea of me.

CHAPTER TEN

Constellations of Pleasure

Pluto, Neptune. Neptune, Pluto. Our two fathers were also brothers. As they were immortal, surely Mother's wasn't the only quim they had both deigned to dip their celestial wicks into. I wonder how many other related whelps they had unceremoniously sired? Brothers begetting brothers. Barring some truly unimaginable mishap, we are the last of our line, at least. I'm pretty sure Mother was past birthing age to give the world another pup. I can't imagine her plumbing, so frequently and consistently plumbed, could host anything more than another watery shot of senatorial sperm. But who knows what happened after I was whisked away from the Baths of Caracalla? Did she mourn me? Did days pass before my absence was even noticed? Did she have the slaves scour the city to see if I had taken up with some pale *pathicus* who had lured me to his home with the promise of a well-stocked library? Not that I dwell on such thoughts. I cannot. Really, my all-empowering thirst is my sole compass. I have no need to ruminate. When these moments arise, it is usually after I have banqueted on a bouquet of cock. Satiated, the mind wanders, but it always loops back to the essential task at hand. Scratch that. Not hand; I rarely use my hands. The essential task at mouth. My impious mouth, needing to be filled, pummeled—a thirst never to be extinguished.

Oh, how the gods dole out their gifts.

Incest came quite naturally to my brother and me. At no point did we have a moment's hesitation, a second thought about using one another's bodies for pleasure. The gods have always fucked each other, fucked their own with a rutting, blind abandon that titillated the mortals who worshiped us, served us, so it makes perfect sense to me that one of us remains to serve *them*. Though it so enraged Father, seeing his son teething on human penis, I can't help but think his response was prophetic. For sometimes, when I travel far into the future, I have no sense of the immortal. I feel, then, that I am the only such being left. Yet loneliness doesn't assail me. I never long for fellow beings. I never flag, for a forest of dick awaits always. I scale them all with my tongue, never looking back, never thinking that my supposedly astonishing lineage makes me too important to grovel. The opposite is true: I grovel *like* a god. All that I give, I give without any thought toward compensation. I give with the kindness that begets worlds and moons, stars even. That work can only be accomplished on your knees.

My travels do seem constrained, as unbelievable as that seems. I sense barely conceivable boundaries. For instance, I rarely call on the bathhouses of ancient Greece and never earlier periods. Likely, none existed prior. Moving forward, if something lies beyond the electric age, with its mesmerizing cell phones and ubiquitous music, I've yet to discover it. One time, however, I did slip though a strange curtain, beads of plastic that dissipated with my touch into silvery sparks of nothingness. Though completely dark, I could somehow see the outline of the men passing through the corridor. All were naked, honed, and muscled. Or not. Each body shape was the perfection of design. Some possessed tiny cocks locked within cages of shocking black light, others sprouted huge, engorged members that shot upward, veritable spears of flesh. This was a new adventure, but one that I was up to, so I joined the groping line of men. Every time the path turned, new subtle scents wafted through the air, laden with nearly indiscernible chemicals. Everyone took rhythmic, deep breaths. Apprehensions melted away. Lust simmered.

In one room, men stood patiently in line, tugging on their cocks or absentmindedly fingering a nipple. Curious, I got in line. The wall before us was lined with large, mouth-like openings. Men stepped into these seemingly organic pink, radiant maws and were immediately swallowed whole. From behind this wall of apertures, I heard orgasmic cries and panting. Before I had time to decide if this was an avenue I wanted to pursue, my turn before the mouth came, the line of men behind me restless, shifting foot to foot, so I stepped in.

A lolling, endless tongue conveyed me forward as the fleshy interior pressed down. Rather than feel claustrophobic, I felt welcomed, embraced, likely the effect of the vapors I continued to be exposed to. Undulating fingers rose from the conveyor-tongue and expertly massaged my shoulders and the soles of my feet. I felt an exploratory nub rub at my ass, and I squeezed my sphincter shut in response while opening my mouth wide, to test just how well this device could intuit my tastes.

A small, probing penis-shaped projectile extended from the surface above and tapped on my tongue, as if it were seeking permission to enter. I nodded assent and gave it a tentative swallow. Sure enough, it stiffened into a more traditional cock shape: the ridged flange, the plump undercarriage of a heavy cock, my favorite contour. So supported in this womblike atmosphere, I curled into a natal ball and teethed and sucked, parting my lips as wide as possible to signal to the machine that I was open to its most advantageous offerings. Soon I felt the head of the simulated penis expand at the slit, so I focused my attention there as a generous amount of ambrosia-like semen flowed forth. The tip of the cock divided in my mouth as it grew, until my tongue was wrestling with a two-headed serpent. The wonder of which elicited a surprising orgasm of my own, which was vacuumed up by a thousand tentacle-like minuscule penises. Normally, I would have worried that the potency of my spunk would gum up the unseen machinery, but I was so comfortable that I stretched and yawned instead, spreading my legs and opening my hands. The funnel responded by playfully lacerating me with countless cock. Elsewhere, I could hear men moan in pleasure, laugh in surprise, cry out in ecstasy. Eventually the lot of us were deposited into a series of interconnected tubs bubbling over with a variety of colors and subtle sensations. This black room was seemingly endless, with men leaping from one pool to another. Though I couldn't sense the ceiling, I imagine anyone looking down would see constellations of pleasure.

Men have their gifts as well.

CHAPTER ELEVEN

The Pounding Hearts of Suns

Obviously, I think a lot about time.

In the past, time was frequently measured by sand. The Egyptians invented the hourglass, or *clepsammia,* as it was called in my youth. We had one in our kitchen. One of my tutors carried it with him from house to house—a large, comical thing to keep his students on task. Sand. Sun-bleached bits of bone and shell ground into fine sediment over the eons. Deserts and beaches are really vast and deep bone yards. And the metaphor is far from apt. If I have learned anything in my travels, it is that time *is* water. Trust me. I know. I follow the flow, expunged from one filthy hollow and into another by oceanic forces. The darkness that presses bone into sand, that greedily clasps the stars, is a tidal thing. That, my friends— and we *are* friends now, right? I mean, we have seen each other naked and all—is what I ride: the aquatic tides of time. The contours, the push and pull of galactic waves, is by now completely familiar to me and yet awe inspiring. Please understand I have tasted it, it clings to my body when I enter whatever new scene I am meant to explore. In addition, just like the sand on the shore, it tastes of salt. The salt limned from countless bodies. Animal into mineral. This is the river of life.

And isn't this what we do with our mouths? Taste what life offers, until we, too, dissipate, and join the loam? Foaming, roaring and then quiet, still and black beneath every star that has existed or will exist.

Therefore, I say to you, new friends, run to the river with me.

❖

Having departed a nondescript, rather barren bathhouse in an unidentifiable era, I again slid through the watery whirlpool of time. Frothy waves pulled me toward my next destination, and even before my wet feet hit the slippery tiled floor, I was elated, having heard the familiar silvery tinkle of what I had long ago been able to identify as "disco" music. I was back. At some point in history, man discovered the ability to capture and record the music of the spheres. The celestial sounds, the circular rhythm of planets and moons and explosive comets, the pounding hearts of suns, were a vibrant part of the bathhouses in New York City and San Francisco. Eventually, these waves of sound became ubiquitous; I knew I had landed in some far future land by how the beat coursing through the air matched the beat of my heart. But of course, my heart beat fastest when I arrived in that new Rome of free men, New York. How that city was lit like the heavens. No wonder these mortals were able to capture and display such vivacious sounds as well. As much as I have marveled at the cultural differences I encounter while traipsing through these glorious grottos, none make me so happy as when I visited the Continental Baths. In a word, these boys know how to party.

❖

Exiting the steam room, I grabbed a dainty, discarded towel and made my way to the dance floor. A gyratory ball of mirrors spewed slivers of throbbing delight across a bouncing bevy of boys and men. The music was both dirty and divine, and it summoned from within my bacchanal desires to dance. Ecstasy swept across every face, some with eyes closed in deep contemplation, others staring toward the silver center of the cosmic orb that spun above. An orgy of movement, of seductive, joyous celebration, the scent of liberated sweat, hands on each other's hips, kissing strangers, lovers, friends, all beneath the glittering rubric of musical joy. For thousands of years prior, the sauna was an escape, and with this new foundation, it became a destination.

I joined in.

I dove into the crowd as if they were the priestesses of my mother's divine cult. How they danced to similar drums, the moon was their disco ball, the flutes and drums commanding their feet in similar fashion. Obsidio and I spied on their midnight ministry from behind the fallen columns of a forgotten temple to Cylene that bordered the family villa in Baiae. I danced. We danced, these men took me up in their arms, hip to hip, we danced, and fingers gracefully traced my shoulders and up and down my spine and soon my towel was off, and an erection bounced against my shimmying ass. I turned to find my suitor tall, a mass of red hair exploding from out of his towel and roaring up his broad chest into a fiery maze. He wore glasses, steamed from the soup of body heat that stewed on the dance floor. He leered down as I stroked his thickening penis through threadbare towel, and he pulled me in the direction of the cabins. However, a younger, handsome man with dark skin put his hand on my shoulder insistently; his lithe form all muscle and movement, the light playing off his body outlined anatomical perfection. My initial paramour, now wide-eyed, quietly begged me to stay on the dance floor. I reached beneath the other towel as well and gave his impressive member a gentle tug. It was slippery and exciting, a silky length of cord I desperately wished for him to drop down my throat slowly, inch by inch. I would dance with them both privately and willed it so. The other man nodded in eager assent. I kept my hands on their cocks as we first wove between the other dancers to join the more elaborate dance within the dark, labyrinthine hallways. Here men posed to impress upon passersby their preferred positions. Cabin doors were opened to reveal men on their stomachs or up on their backs, legs spread. Men all ready to mount or be mounted. The air was thick with the fog of amyl nitrate and beery breath, with a lingering undercurrent of semen cooling on the sticky cement floor. Both men kept close with me in between, as if I were a prisoner being marched to his cell, and the slim room *was* cell-like. An amber light bulb lent a dusky battlefield air to the confined quarters as we piled in and shut the door behind us. I squatted down, planning to spend my time pivoting back and forth between the serpents released before me, but as I licked Red's shaft, Night leaned over my head to kiss Red, who returned the kiss with a surprised fervor. Night lifted me up and placed the head of his cock within the notch of my now-spread legs. I wrapped my arms around Red's waist as his penis plunged down my throat and Night entered me from behind. As their parries and thrusts found a rhythm within my being, I felt as if their sword tips might clash, igniting internal sparks that would fly out of the corners of my eyes, choked out from around the large muscle filling my mouth, drip from my nose and pool on the floor like moonlight on still waters. Night possessed my ass, spitting on his dick any time enough of the length was exposed. He maneuvered me just so. My feet hung over the curve of his shoulders and so I was levitated.

Sweat dripped from Night's forehead, and Red's moss-like pubic hair was in my eyes so I could not properly look up, but I heard the men continue to kiss and share a bottle of poppers. Our tripled body heat, the music filtering in through the door's edges, expounded on the rhythm of the men entering me in tandem. As a suspended Icarus, I melted feather by feather, falling away into a torrid wax that the men before and behind me used to lather and join their forms, painting us into one hot being, a solar thing, beneath the earth but about to break out. With that, Red's semen issued forth while Night poured himself into my ass. I pulled both of their fluids into me, a reverse volcano of molten hunger. Both men let out a cry and fell into the other, pressing me closer to their slick bodies. Night's cock fell out as Red twitched and went limp across my tongue. I dropped to my knees and turned, thrilled to finally take Night into my mouth, to clean his hot length with my tongue, all while alternately turning to nip and suck at the head of Red lest he feel out of favor. However, Night came back, as night always does, and his full girth compressed my tongue as his blunt thumbs stretched my lips and I nursed his penis slowly, lovingly, with a cadence to match the beautiful music pulsing from outside.

❖

The steam room is practically empty. A favorite singer has taken the stage, and the men and boys all rushed to crowd around her, Red and Night front and center, singing along. The wet tendrils of time loop around my wrists, tempting me to withdraw and reappear in another such establishment. But I resist. Simply by standing up and casually switching seats, I can stave off transport. Music seeps in as the door opens and a tired, satiated soul joins me. An older man, well-tanned, gold chains draped across a wide chest bounding with silvery hair. He sighs as he reclines on the wooden bench beside me. His towel parts, and his limp, extended penis dangles from beneath his large belly. He doesn't bother to pull on it as I reposition myself between his legs. I can tell this organ has received quite the workout already, so I sit and admire it, absently stroking the tufts of hair encircling his ankles. He relaxes more as a fresh burst of steam consumes both of us. We are mere heated shadows, conjoined by the lightest of touches. Whenever I feel that portal of steam opening, compelling me to leave, I dismiss it by shifting from one foot to the other. Soon this man's penis will need my attention, and after the singer takes her last bow, men will come, patiently lining up, gossiping, flexing in the mirror, all waiting for their turn on my tongue.

Yes, the Continental Baths, too, is also one of my favorite shores on which to land.

CHAPTER TWELVE

Pausanias Made Richer

I was a lover of books before I was a lover of men.

Our lone family trip to Greece was a marvelous adventure for my young mind: to see where the heroes of my scrolls had trod, battled, consummated affairs with no scant number of demure boys and portent women, all while assuming an unusual variety of animal shapes. Mother was both amused and angry when she realized I had packed nearly the entirety of my personal library, the plan being I would just wash and wear a single toga, so as to have my scrolls at hand to verify historical data and the like. The slaves repacked my bags, and I was allowed a single copy of Hesiod, *The Works*, as approved by my sternest, most drab new tutor. Obsidio, in a rare show of sympathy, packed his copy of Pausanias, famous for his travel writings detailing the Seven Wonders of the World and more, knowing I would pore over it at each stop.

Mother had planned a far-from-ambitious tour. A languid cruise to a handful of islands that mattered, more time in Athens than the typical tourist allots, a side trip to see the sibyls that was destined to be canceled, but I was thrilled, to say the least. The idea that I would have days to explore the libraries of the university more than made up for the loss of my scrolls. Though in overhearing her gossip with a friend over wine late one evening, I was able to discern that the real motivation for the trip was the rumored size of the oars that swung between the legs of the sailors navigating the ship Mother had booked for the voyage. In fact, later I learned at the Baths of Caracalla while licking the paddle of one such seaman that once the tour operator had gotten wind of this rumor, he only hired cooks, entertainers, and seamen who were thus equipped, guaranteeing bored and wealthy matrons would fill his Grecian cruises to capacity, even in the off-season. So while the staff plugged Mother's holes, I was free to traverse the deck of the boat, which bore the ghastly name of *Trimalchio's Feast*, constantly scouting the horizons for sea monsters. I looked for distant islands bespeckled with statues and temples of note, hoping that maybe, just maybe, the form of my father would pass beneath—a celestial shadow that the mere mortal would think a robust school of fish, but with a touch of his ichor in my veins, I would know that it was him, expressing fatherly concern for one of his many offspring. I stared hard at the sea, until the sun reflecting off the waves hurt my eyes. My neck was hot, the boards beneath my bare feet rough, unsteady. I was unsure if he was actually down there or up on Mount Olympus, though either way, I had no proof he was concerned about my whereabouts. Neptune had uncountable children. I was but one minnow in a vast school of fish, a shred of shadow, a meager droplet of the prodigious seed he had spewed across eternity.

Obsidio's battered copy of Pausanias was made richer by the dueling notes of two previous owners. One was a dry, overly intellectual student from the Stoic school. The other was a rather randy tutor traveling on the cheap, forever belittling the notes of his newfound foe and traveling companion, as well as scribbling in the margins humorously culinary descriptions of the wide variety of ass he screwed on his grand tour. His offhand description of every hole he plundered caused a tightening in the lap of my toga far different from the erections I woke up with every morning. This I could purposely incite and thrilled in doing so, for this was before my dual discoveries of incest and the baths, so scrolls were my only erotic outlet. I stole the scroll from Obsidio's luggage as frequently as I could. Barred from Mother's room, which reverberated with panting and moaning, the cramped bathroom below deck barely afforded any privacy, so I was forced to read out in the open, doing everything I could in order to disguise my burgeoning erection. My titillating travels in literature alit upon an exciting fact. Near the house we had rented in Athens was an unremarkable cemetery where an unmarked grave was believed to hold the remains of Aristogeiton. This hero, along with his lover Harmodius, had slain a tyrant. Harmodius was killed on the spot while Aristogeiton was tortured for his role. Men who loved men long made pilgrimage to this grave in hopes that paying respect would reward them with a brave companion of their own. Both the student and the tutor had visited. However, while the student dryly recorded a description of the hero's grave, remarking that it was sad commentary on today's society that their story was on its way to being forgotten, the tutor noted that after sunset men gathered among the tombstones for secret assignations. He had himself bent a small Assyrian over our champion's tomb and fucked him while other Greeks and assorted tourists gathered to watch. I was driven to distraction by the idea of hiding behind a sepulcher and watching men touch other men. I wanted to touch some myself.

That first night in Athens, I exaggerated my excitement concerning the next day's tour schedule, driving my mother to distraction until, exasperated, she banished me to my room for the remainder of the evening. I immediately took to the window and scurried out, down into the dusty street. Athens was different from Rome. Its older, more compact streets were thick with refuse and dogs. The cemetery was beside our rented house, its stone wall low and crumbling. Even before entering, I could see the solitary silhouette of a man prowling about within. Heart pounding, sweat from my brow stinging my eyes, I jumped the wall and landed unevenly on a grave that had collapsed inward into a weedy mix of soil and bone. The sounds from the frantic Athenian streets were somehow muffled by the preponderance of graves and winding cypress trees. Like those tombs along the Appian Way, these attempts at one last clamor for immortality succeeded largely on the largesse available at the time of passing. Huge monuments crowded out less impressive graves, those deemed more austere by the pocketbook rather than any philosophical leanings of the departed. Statuary told silent tales of ancestral respect or desertion, primarily by the amount of bird shit cresting their noble foreheads or exposed crowns. I stumbled out of the shallow pit and looked around for coupling men, hoping the darkness would invite closer inspections of what I had so far only caught faraway glimpses of at wrestling matches or slave auctions.

The lanes were straightforward but unkempt, so I moved slowly across the uneven cobblestone and bits of broken masonry hidden within rising shafts of brittle weeds and parched grass. A figure moved about in the distance. *Where are the others?* The guidebook scribe had promised a horde of hungry men. *Maybe I'm too early?* Fear and lust, newly conjoined twins fused at the foreskin, drove me forward. My throat was dry. A modest erection bobbed between my legs like a divining rod. I could not see the man I was after but sensed he had entered a jumble of high tombs, fenced by bricked enclosures to mark family plots. I could no longer see the wall I had jumped over. This was a silent place of stillness and death. The urge to flee mounted as the figure I was following emerged nearby. He stood upon a tomb to survey the cemetery. His sinewy silhouette beneath the moon revealed that he was a youth as well. My fear subsided and desire built as I realized he was naked in the moonlight. The upward curve of his solid penis pulled me forward. I guessed that, like me, he was disappointed in just how unpopulated the graveyard was with the nocturnal living. I rushed forward through the maze and tripped on a short burst of uneven, weedy stairs. I fell into an open grave, landing softly on fresh soil that, though my fall was cushioned, knocked the breath out of me.

He swooped down, a ravenous vulture. Expertly pinning my thin wrists together with one bony hand, with his other he ripped my toga off. I thrashed about, but he bade me be quiet with a familiar head butt that signaled more pain was in order if I was not compliant.

Obsidio slid his thick member between my thighs and grunted in satisfaction as I reluctantly parted my sweaty legs.

Obsidio.

I knew him by his breath. No matter the tongue scraping, the scented rinse, he exuded a whiff of the underworld. His breath held the dankness of a sealed tomb. There was a hint of buried decay. And as he matured, his darkness emerged in other ways. He could disappear when crossing into a shadow. His dismissive laugh lowered the temperature in small rooms. As his penis poked and prodded my thighs, he bit down hard on my exposed neck, more to elicit a whimper and demonstrate his mastery over me than any other reason.

He grunted and whispered, "Do you like my big worm, little bookworm? I am going to put it inside you. I hope it does not cut through your guts too much, though you've certainly landed in the right place if this is something we only get to do once."

He flipped me over and pushed my legs farther apart with his sharp knees. He spat into the palm of his hand and inserted a dirty finger into my virgin hole. I tried to scream, but he shoved my face into the black dirt. A broken garland of faded flowerings rung around my skull as he attempted entry. With one hand, he brushed away at the dirt before my face to reveal a cold, pale visage. As my brother's weight pushed me forward, I realized what I had thought was fallen statuary was the corpse of a boy. He appeared to be around my age. Our motion caused one of the worn coins to slip from his eyes. His lids indolently parted to reveal cold quartz, reflecting the jaundice of the full moon.

Obsidio forced his way inside me, and I struggled to push him out and found that in doing so I could grip him, and that this internal grip was inviting. *I want just this thing*. The cold dirt and clammy belly of the boy beneath pressed against my exposed cock, which lengthened, much to my horror.

"Yes, brother. Open up to me."

I felt all of him inside me, stretching me to new capacities with his brutal thrusting, wild, without rhythm. Blind progress burned, and I felt suffocated by his weight, yet elevated by the pain and pleasure burrowing within. The body beneath me rocked in unison with us, a sick marionette to our incestuous copulation. I could hear the teeth of the lifeless corpse grimly click together, almost as if they were chattering on a cold night. Death *is* carnal. Obsidio was, after all, his father's son.

His sperm shot through me like hot arrows, and I came, too. I convulsed in delirium as he pulled out and wiped the dripping miasma of shit, sperm, and soil from his still-hard cock onto the shreds of my toga.

I blinked away the tears and rolled over on my back, looking about wildly for an escape. We were in an appropriately narrow grave. Obsidio must have scouted the location beforehand and balanced himself on the brick enclosure, to give the illusion he was standing atop a covered tomb. He pushed himself off me and jumped out.

"Looks like I owe dear old Pausanias a bit of thanks, eh?"

He stood and sneered down at me, pulling his toga from atop the statue of a weeping maiden, an empty bird's nest precariously placed within the nook of her cracked arms.

I blinked, not understanding, unsure of why I felt so much pleasure mixed with dread.

He left without another word, without so much as a look back. As I lay in the dirt, anger rose within me. And it was not directed at him. I was angry at myself for wondering when we could do it again.

❖

I washed in the murky waters of a fountain in the middle of the cemetery. I did not fully understand Obsidio's final utterance until I returned to reading Pausanias that next morning. My body felt stretched and twisted, used and yet somehow new, ready. When I walked across the room, I knew my gait was different, that aspects of my manhood had been revealed, the permutations of hot destiny stirred. I returned to the scroll, ready to read more of the ongoing argument between the previous two travelers as much as the words of the master himself, but their conversation stopped at the cemetery. Perplexed, I unrolled the additional texts, but the margins were unmarked. It had all been a ruse by Obsidio. A masterful forgery to lure me out of the house, to a place where he could take me regardless of how much I cried out.

Death is carnal, a carnal trap.

CHAPTER THIRTEEN

Shared Seas

Every time I come ashore—for in many ways these are my beaches, time my tide—wherever I land, I understand what the men are saying. I am aware there is a difference among the languages spoken, and it saddens me to no small degree that Greek is no longer the language of court, and Latin has multiplied and mutated in several forked, interlocking and serpentine tongues. However, wherever I am, I know what is being said, and I can speak just as fluently. I have decided this is an inherited trait and not an unstated condition of my inimitable travels. My father could talk to fish. All sea creatures obeyed his command. I once overheard Mother tell Obsidio that whenever he whispered in her ear, he sounded like a porpoise, which caused her to immediately convulse in climax. (I am convinced that she shared her more disturbing sexual secrets with him purely to elicit that rarest of reactions: a smile). As I can breathe underwater, so too it is likely I also possess his ability to communicate with a vast variety of living things, an ability that has transformed into an aptitude to understand what men of different eras, countries, and continents say within the confines of our shared seas.

In my initial sensual delirium—and I do mean I was

absolutely *mad* for cock—I hardly noticed that men alone populated the bathhouses as I leapfrogged from one steamy location to the next. After perhaps a century of being enchanted by penises, I had a moment of supine reflection within a relaxing bubble bath that I did, indeed, have a past. *All of these men!* The scope and breadth of my curse took hold, and my mind began to entertain certain notions: that at some point men started to begat men, so women had vanished. In addition, I noticed that some rather large men had admirers. Were these men then pregnant? Was there competition to claim the offspring or some social advantage in helping to raise the whelps? It took a while to sort these things out, though not as long to understand that the Roman Empire did not die, it shattered.

Europa was drastically changed. After Londinium rose and fell, another empire adopted the royal purple and spun it into red, white, and blue. This "America" is, as far as I can tell, vast, a continent unknown in my youth. And, like Rome, it did not seem to deliver on many of its promises, but the music that its deep sorrows rutted out of certain souls made the Grecian experiment a worthy one, I suppose. And poor, raisin-like Greece. Rarely did I hear the mellifluous language, except when I was actually in Greece, and the strictures of my sojourns never afforded me many visits to the periods I would have preferred. I never got the opportunities to meet the philosophers I had so much admired, though in the lustful frenzy of my travels, would I have asked any of them the right questions? My mute mouth fixed on their penises, my eyes transfixed upon brows containing singular truths and jewel-like thoughts I only wish I could tap as easily and expertly as I draw semen from the cock.

So. I have rarely seen a woman in these labyrinths. The newspapers that occasionally skirt across my path have detailed political progress. I seldom find books, owing to the temperament of these various dens and labyrinths as much as the moisture in the air, not to say their very purpose does not lend itself to academic pursuits. In certain, wondrous eras where music permeates the baths, I hear sonic sirens, beloved by a head-bobbing many. But due to my thirst, it interests me more that these men are so dedicated to other men that they have thrown off the yoke of heritage and familial reproductive duty. I only hear disembodied voices; the stories and lives of my Sapphic sisters are hidden from me as well.

In a tired, world-weary ephebe with hollow eyes, I occasionally hear the hollow laugh of my mother.

❖

I do see love here. Men fall in love within the baths. Sometimes for a few minutes or several hours, an endless night both parties will remember for the rest of their lives. And I do mean love, not lust. There is a difference about the eyes, an alteration in the kiss, a lightness that blossoms in the heart never to fully fade.

There are men who have only known love in the baths. My travels once took me to a bathhouse in London, an evolved Londinium, no longer a dingy port town harried by Celts and mangy werewolves, but a teeming capital. I witnessed a young, sheepish man take his first step inside such an establishment. I could feel the trepidation from the locker room, and I peered around a corner to see. He was too frightened to move, however, and an older gentleman with a thick mustache was buzzed in and nearly knocked him over. Quickly assessing the youngster's state, he offered an assured pat on the arm and said, "Here, here. You just need a jolly good steam."

The older man chatted him up as they disrobed, and

he gave him a tour of the facilities as if it were just another gymnasium, greatly setting the boy at ease. Their chaste kiss in the steam room was an affectionate beginning. When I found myself back at the same bathhouse in what must have been a decade later, little had changed. However, there the couple was again, older, obviously settled into a habit of meeting there at an appointed set date and time. They played cards in their towels in a little sitting area and shared tea and a tin of biscuits and chatted about their children. I overheard the younger man excitedly share every detail about his newborn, while his older friend, shorn of mustache but thicker in belly, nodded and chirped appreciative noises. A few passing men clutched their towels and scowled at their jovial exchange, as if this sharing broke some unspoken pact. I swam through time, surfacing across the globe and again returned; what felt like only a fortnight to me had passed, and there they were, much older. Now the younger one was helping the older man at the door. He had a cane and was much pained in disrobing. I sensed an unspoken agreement the arrangement would not hold much longer. The sauna was empty but possessed an air of tension and foreboding. They spoke of a great war, of how facilities such as this were being commandeered for use as makeshift hospitals or to put to use by bivouacking troops.

Within white curtains of steam that folded and unfolded, I observed their final kiss, a passion meant to swallow time was itself about to be devoured, and they accepted this fate. Then I heard the younger one whisper in his lover's ear, "There he is again. I tell you that's the same little faun I spied the day we met. And again all those years later, when we played spades that winter the Thames froze over. He's here to bid us farewell. See him there? I told you our meetings were magic."

The older man looked over at me, but not really at me, more over my shoulder, toward a place of promise that even my immortal self could not see. They held hands and repeated little jokes long unmoored of their original meanings but still of familiar comfort. They kissed. Tears intermingled as they pulled one another into the shadows for a last embrace. I leaned back and let the steam take me wherever I was meant to travel, feeling a bit warmer than usual.

So yes, I do see love here.

CHAPTER FOURTEEN

Darkest Marvel

Outside erotic excursions, of all the varied experiences I have had since my aquatic expulsion, few have been as astonishing as the discovery of soap. Soap. These ponderous white bricks fit in the palm of your hand, yet add a spray of water and a vigorous rub and a veritable waterfall of sparkling suds results. Endless silvery liquid excretions drip like luxuriant honey from foggy containers mounted alongside rusted spigots. Soap and the delirious molecules therein that expand into popping wet galaxies of bubbles—truly these ninth wonders of the world nearly rival the electricity that has ubiquitously replaced candlelight and oil lamps. Oh, the cascade of revelations that followed in terms of cleanliness.

We Romans assumed that we had not only invented hygiene, we had developed exquisite practices and rituals that were the very apex of civilization. If I were to reveal the habits we considered acceptable to my latter-day bathhouse denizens, the world would balk. Compared to the savage Visigoths harrying our farthest borders, for whom every tree was a toilet, we thought using a shared sponge on a stick to wipe our asses after shitting, or the aforementioned strigil, used to scrape our skins clean, was sophisticated. We thought our luxurious heated pools separated us from the half-human beasts that lurked about on the edges of Numidian deserts. Well, the cascade of shampoos, deodorants, and black combs preserved in iridescent blue liquid glistening beneath the neon lights of tiled bathrooms lined with private stalls replete with toilets, porcelain oysters that gingerly swallowed excrement with the simple toggle of a handle, all overwhelmed and humbled what we once considered cosmopolitan.

Ironically, I discovered my first such toilet in some future Rome. I knew the city from the smell of the Tiber alone. And the men by their noses and the familiar, coarse tufts of hair regally at rest, like epaulets on their relaxed shoulders. It was a wonder to see the same statuesque figures and recognize centuries later the descendants of the same louche prostitutes, filling similar doorways, nursing the same larcenous desperation that had narrowed souls while ballooning biceps.

Yet another unthinkable convenience in that distant past that considered itself the pinnacle of sanitation, some saunas were fitted with little silver stalls that contained coils of cords ready to unleash a forceful spray with which nimble boys cleansed their holes, always after soaping up the opening with an exploratory finger. Other establishments possessed water fountains that dispensed mint-infused water to better refresh stretched and abused mouths. But what era does not fancy itself that high point of progress, never knowing future generations will look back over their washed, scrubbed, depilated shoulders with a dismissive laugh. The bouquet of endless scents, the silky textures, this godly effluence, lubricated my journey and made every shower room a potential miniature Olympus, with clouds of foam like white topiary slowly sliding down broad, tanned chests to land atop my head. And there I am on my knees again before a throng of Titans, their lathered shafts waiting for the crucial swab of my tongue.

Roman women and some of the more effeminate men wore perfume, so we *were* acquainted with the finer scents civilization afforded. Mother would take us on the occasional shopping excursion to the *Graecostadium* near the Forum. There was a discreet alley stocked with merchants who peddled expensive perfumes and rare cosmetics from every corner of the empire. Typically, Mother assigned household shopping to one of the kitchen slaves, but she preferred to pick out her own cosmetics. Her morning and evening routines were elaborate rituals that required more ointments and unguents than one would have thought possible, all with the help of a diminutive *cosmetae*, a silent acne-scarred Persian slave whose sole duty was to assist in the application and removal of layer after layer of preservation.

Like all upper-class women, Mother valued fair skin above all else. I believe she managed these excursions on her own because she did not want the slaves to know how much chalk and other skin whitening makeup she purchased, nor the amount she was willing to spend on such items. I recall her paying one specific merchant within a regal tent clouded with frankincense an exorbitant sum for the desiccated dung of an albino crocodile. I occasionally accompanied her and was allotted some coin to spend at the booksellers if I behaved. Her definition of behaving was to be completely quiet as she absorbed every word of the intricate instructions on the application of whatever powder had just been unpacked that morning off the latest ship from Alexandria.

Perseus was charged with keeping me out of the way while Mother shopped. He feigned indifference, but I knew he coveted her creams. During the holiday of *Saturnalia,* when slaves were permitted to disrespect their masters, he put on an annual show at dinner by donning her stola and painting his face as hers in a mockery that she coolly enjoyed. She, in turn, was far more familiar with the slaves during that one day, pouring Perseus the best wine, dutifully applying makeup to her little *cosmetae* until she shone like a freshly chiseled statue of the most ethereal marble. The slave-child was beautiful, but the alabaster application would fissure if she smiled, making her into a crone. Mother always asked the younger slaves what presents they would each like during *Sigillaria*, the day of gift-giving that soon followed. When I was old enough to hoist a pitcher, I participated as well, serving the kitchen slaves and pretending to whimper and cry as they lobbed tender criticisms at my performance and delivered mock beatings.

I tugged at the end of Perseus's tunic to indicate I wanted to explore more of the market. He was hesitant but obeyed. Both of us knew my mother could spend hours hanging on every word these tradesmen uttered, deliberating between noxious creams that promised youthful pallor and nocturnal elixirs that erased wrinkles. The bustle and excitement of the alleys and myriad shops were all precursors to the dominant business at hand: the slave market.

The *Graecostadium* was Rome's largest, oldest slave market, erected to move the massive amount of human capital from the long-ago conquering of Greece. This was a gloomy place of the rawest commerce, where men, women, and children stood for sale, naked and silent on rotating platforms. The defeated, the kidnapped, the multitude born into slavery, the sold and resold—all weary links in the human chain that pulled the Roman economy ever forward. That this gleaming empire raked the world over, capturing entire cities, upending families, pulling babes from the arms of their mothers, and never felt itself tarnished by such acts is the darkest marvel.

Children fetched a low amount, being a burden on the owner until they were trained and of age to add value to the purchasing household. Pity those who went to the mines or the galley ships. Their short lives of pure drudgery stood in absolute contrast to those bought up by wealthy households. Some of the rich in Rome put even our family to shame. Their wealth was so abundant, with vast estates across the provinces manned by hundreds of slaves. These servants had living quarters and lifestyles that far exceeded anything the typical laboring freedman in Rome could ever expect. After decades of service, they were often rewarded with their freedom and quaint farms on which to retire, complete with slaves of their own. Their fate hinged entirely on who bought them, whether the wealthiest thought to send an agent to the market, whether the mines of the damned had a specific order to fill and needed more hands. I observed them all. A placard hung from their neck listing skills, attributes, languages spoken, country of origin, and, most importantly, price.

Our family was wealthy enough that slavers brought their chattel directly to our house for private viewing, so any bartering could be done indoors and the sales tax quietly overlooked. I took every chance to steal away to this section of the market so I could satisfy my burgeoning curiosity for cock. Here I could stare far more openly, wantonly, than at the baths or by examining the small numbers paraded through our portico before my watchful mother at home. I rushed through the crowd toward the area where the gladiatorial slaves were displayed. These naked beasts stood proud or defeated, dim-witted or conniving. Regardless their disposition, they were exposed, and I stood still, studying their cocks as if every sinew and vein was a line of powerful verse I needed to commit to memory to please a demanding but righteous tutor.

Perseus chatted with a neighbor's slave while I took census of the flaccid cocks that rotated before the crowd. Young, old, some shriveled and withdrawn, tucked within an agitated pubic tangle, others protruded like plump purple gourds, minor miracles of human anatomy ripe for closer inspection. I was relieved all eyes were on the slaves so I could just gape, each penis a unique marvel I measured and caressed with my eyes. I was only just beginning to imagine what I would do with such fleshy treasures if given the appropriate latitude. Within my room at night, I curled up caressing myself with forbidden dreams of serving the servants, only to wake with my thighs slick with nascent semen.

"Nerites. Funny to find you here, funnier still how we look at the same thing and yet see such differences."

The cold hand that rested on my shoulder was matched by the chilly timbre of my brother's voice.

Nerites. He spoke my name so casually you would think we chatted like this in the marketplace all the time. Often, we went weeks without speaking. He could go a year without uttering my name. Sure, he spoke to me all the time with his condemnatory eyes, with a dismissive brush of his hand. Nothing but disdain had passed between us for years, not that it bothered me. I certainly didn't feel special for it; he appeared to hate everyone. Everyone but Mother, who, though she certainly did not dote on him, gave him everything he wanted within reason. They held each other in a kind of mutual respect. Predators of a difference species who nonetheless admired one another's methodology. So to hear him speak my name, nonchalantly, in public even…a reflexive shiver ran up my spine. Obsidio tightened his grip on my shoulder.

"Nerites, it's not cold out, yet you are practically quaking. Lean back into me for warmth," he cooed.

I obeyed and felt the coarseness of his new toga envelop my gooseflesh-pricked skin. His erection pressed against the small of my back, and I gasped. This was the first penis I had ever touched other than my own, and I had been wrestling with my small member every evening and some afternoons of late, always wishing it belonged to another, squeezing my eyes shut to better imagine the glorious cocks swinging between the legs of renowned gladiators, the cuter tutors, and some of the sturdier slaves that carried my mother's palanquin. When my eyes were closed their tightest, the deepest, darkest part of my mind's hidden ocean offered up furtive glimpses of Neptune from when I was a mere babe in my wet nurse's arms. He sat before us naked, legs parted while my mother knelt before him, his prodigious member flaccid yet powerful, practically breathing in her hands. Even then, I wanted to trade her balmy milk for his…

Obsidio's warmth spread through the toga and pulsed against my back. Now both of his hands were on my shoulders to steady me as he slowly, imperceptibly, ground his penis into my back. Before us, a gladiator-slave raised his shackled hands and let out a roar. A gaggle of prospective buyers clucked their approval. Emboldened, the slave leapt into the throng of people and head-butted an off-duty centurion who happened to be making his way through the crowd. The soldier looked as if he had just woken up in a brothel, hungover and robbed of his money, so this final indignity was the last straw.

As he stumbled back up, he unsheathed his sword, likely the gladiator's intended goal. The slave leapt to action and deftly relieved the surprised warrior of his weapon. Wild-eyed, laughing that his plan had come to fruition, the slave swung the sword wide to part the crowd, which whooped in excitement, knowing that the Praetorian Guard would soon descend from their respective posts and give them a free show. However, several large, glum slavers encircled the escapee, cracking their furious black whips. The gladiator turned his head to and fro, unsure which attacker was the weak link, all while whips slashed his face and arms.

As each line of blood opened across his cheek, Obsidio

thrust into my back. His stiffness was incomparable, like flesh turned bludgeon. I shuddered with each lethal snap of the whip. There we stood as the man faltered and dropped his sword and the slavers closed in. Obsidio's grip tightened as his heated cock fused into my backside, my toga now drenched in our commingled sweat. The crowd that had gathered dispersed at the bark of the arriving Praetorian Guard. Their helmets masked their anger at having their afternoon duties interrupted. The slavers parted as the first soldier drew his sword and with one practiced move decapitated the now exhausted, confused, and battered would-be fugitive.

As his severed head tumbled to the ground, awash in a spurting eruption of blood, Obsidio bucked and stabbed at my back. His hot orgasm raced up my spine and pricked the hollow between my shoulder blades. He eased his grip. My knees practically buckled as I wetted my own lap with an intense orgasm, my first initiated by the touch of another. Perseus, who had been cowering behind a column, rushed to my side, grabbed my hand, and tried to pull me away. But I remained wedded to my brother, desperate for our bond to remain, for us to grow into Romulus and Remus feeding on one another. But as I looked up longingly into his eyes, he did not return my hungry stare. He looked elsewhere, down into the ground. I followed his gaze and saw that he was lost in the dark, widening pool of blood spilling forth from the collapsed pucker of the dead slave's oozing neck.

I again looked up at him, trying to decipher his terrible concentration.

"What do you see, brother?" I managed to whisper, Perseus clawing at my slender wrists.

"My own reflection."

Our slave finally managed to pull me away. As we pushed through the crowd, I looked back over my shoulder. Obsidio did not even notice my absence. He could not tear himself away from the black shimmer of blood emanating from the emptied body. The arc of Obsidio's erection was clearly visible through his semen-slicked toga. The slaves on the rotating slabs ignored the corpse at their feet and instead trained their unfocused gaze up into the cloudy distance.

CHAPTER FIFTEEN

Useless Lucre

The sauna was small, dank, subterranean, and familiar. I was back in Japan, thankful to have surfaced at one of the few bathhouses where I maintain a locker, affording me the convenience of discreetly relieving myself. As an immortal, I do not require normal sustenance to survive, though I will enjoy the occasional beer when in a European sauna, if the mood strikes. However, my predilection for penis often requires that I swallow. During multiple encounters, it is practically required. There is a certain etiquette to orgies. The symphony cannot come to a halt simply because the conductor needs to cough, so to speak. Too many instruments are in play. Plus, I love how the webbing of intermingled semen coalesces on my tongue, lubricating the roof of my mouth. This wet, interlaced tunnel transforms me into an even finer instrument. Surely the ichor coursing in my veins is now wholly white—the milk of all the men I have sucked makes me a well in reverse.

And a deep one at that.

❖

Some elderly men reposition themselves within a fog of whispers and rustling newspaper as I exit. The bathroom has a convenient douching station and, after securing the door, I squat over my cupped hand and, with a stifled grunt, squeeze out a clutch of greasy pearls.

Washing them beneath the hose suspended against the wall, I cannot help but examine this futile treasure. The largest pearl glistens mischievously, drawing in all of what dim light illuminates the stall. I pop it in my mouth and roll it around on my tongue like a portentous grape, and sure enough, I soon recognize the taste of an amazing Swede who had populated my throat several months ago. The blond fuzz of his thighs was a forest of delight. I teethed on pleasant memories while I headed back to the locker room.

A *yakuza* straddling a bench watched me while smoking a cigarette. A Japanese gangster, easily identified by the tattoos marching up his back and rushing down his thick arms, a taboo in Japanese polite society. I only see this exquisite art when I emerge in saunas reserved for this "criminal class." Though in temperance and physicality, I do not see much difference between them and the samurai I had sucked off in earlier eras. He was brutish, short, his towel parted so the terrapin head of his rigid penis poked through a pubic torrent as black and luxuriant as freshly dyed raw silk. I nodded ever so slightly, eager to return and serve him, but first I needed to attend to business.

Next, I smiled and offered a deferential bow to the *mama-san* folding towels. She covered her mouth and giggled. We recognized each other, having passed in the halls over the eons. She had been handing me towels for centuries, and I knew her to be a fox in human form. At first, I had wondered if she, too, was cursed to live life among humans locked within this particular sauna. Judging from the boots and coats some of the men shrugged off, they were in a cold part of Japan, but she toiled so effortlessly, whispering so genially with the regulars, that had I come to regard her as a simple steam-spirit happy to be indoors and content with her work. I was always pleased whenever I surfaced at this bathhouse. The proximity to this kindred being was as soothing as the massive, steeping soaking tubs that consumed the bathing area. Fortunately, this was a frequent, welcome stop on the tides of my journey, and thus a perfect repository for my pearls.

I spun the knob on the locker to and fro, the date of Obsidio's birthday dancing from my fingertips. I opened the door cautiously, fearful I would unleash a rolling flood of pearls, a bouncing cascade of various shapes and sizes, all a milky hue of silver and white. The gangster had followed me. I gave him a hard, long stare, and the blush of his turtle-cock hardened into a shiny, purplish bruise. He jerked his head toward the cavernous steam room. I had spent uncountable hours on my knees in there, lost in a shimmering fog of heat and occasional body contact. I nodded my agreement and spat the pearl that had been wallowing in my mouth out into my palm. This movement always recalled the childhood game of knucklebones. Then we played for favorite toys or our pocket money. Now I am slowly amassing a horde of useless lucre I could never spend. But so what? I am charity, I am a funnel of thirst, I am another whorl in the twisting steam within a dark room where, in my best, most lucid moments, I cannot find the walls or even the floor. I am so lost in revelry.

I followed the *yakuza* in, to greedily rob him of his teeming sperm. He hung his towel on a peg by the door and stood still, allowing me to admire the inked forms exploding out of his muscled back and racing up and down his arms and legs. His buttocks were well developed, so I knelt and began kissing each tough cheek. He grunted assent and parted his legs just so, and my tongue found the hard knot of his ass as a fresh blast of steam enveloped us both. I licked his crack and wormed my way between his legs until my tongue was as far up his hole as it could go, his firm testicles riding my sweaty forehead. He grunted again, and I intuited this as the command to serve his cock, so I quickly pivoted and began sucking the salty tip. He pushed his way in between my lips as I lapped at his tumescence. My own erection swatted his ankles, keeping rhythm with my mouth. Rivers of steam unwound throughout the room, revealing a small audience. Some watched intently, admiring my technique. Others opened their towels to display ready erections, signaling that they, too, would appreciate my service. His thigh muscles tensed. I tongued the veiny ridge that ran along the base of his penis. A final grunt. I swallowed.

I eased back onto my bare buttocks as he stepped away. The only sound was of breathing men and hissing steam. Ingesting his hot ejaculate, I willed it downward to better plant these slick globules within the folds of my bowels. There both time and my distinctive chemistry will massage some remaining kernel into a bright pearl, one that will hopefully reflect the sharp crescent of the malice in his eyes.

CHAPTER SIXTEEN

These Beasts Live to Conquer

How I love the animals among us. These beast-men who lumbered past whatever domestication process exists in their society to fuck with complete abandon. And they are just *completely* beasts, all unfettered appetite, with dog dicks and a gnarl of coarse pubic hair, legs of scarred and twisted muscle, foul buttocks, clawlike feet, and rough hands that hold my skull as if it were a stolen chalice meant to piss in. You cannot call them selfish, for they possess no recognition of the other—all of the world is a but a plaything, a bevy of receptacles bent to receive their pleasure. These beasts live to conquer, to fuck, to eat and drink, to take full, hearty clockwork-like shits and then back to work, work being pummeling any available ass or mouth.

This is not to say that I do not enjoy intellectuals. Conversations about music, theater, philosophy, these are rare joys, and when given the opportunity to partake, I revel. Of course, I need to be a good listener, as I'm somewhat uninformed concerning the goings on in the world outside, and the political landscape shifts just as much as my locale and era, so I have to be careful of what I repeat and have developed a very keen ear for the vernacular. It should be noted multitudes of personalities take to the baths, some of them quite twisted in their desires. Some such incubi I do hold a grudge against, for they are the very opposite of the beast-men who stuff my mouth and rear. For the first couple of eons, I was a bit of a kappa in how I treated the men with malice in their hearts. The beasts here have a sexual conceit that is oceanic, something to relax into, but the creatures formed from spite, either born rotten or misshaped by a world that judges their desire as fetid, these twisted insects have a point to drive home, and they use the saunas less as erotic playgrounds and more as cheerless prisons within which to reenact the repetitive plays that populate the empty theaters of their desiccated minds. These are the men who keep their bodies in good shape more so they can judge their peers than to maintain health. The bathhouses are an important and necessary stage for them. Like spiders, they need a web to attract witless flies. They find each other and gossip, and they entice their victims and withdraw just when the other is on the precipice of pleasure. These spider queens occupy pathetic thrones in every era, and I used to trip them in the shower. Occasionally, I would steal their partners—entice them away, to the great relief of their original trick. I did this for decades before I finally realized that you cannot thwart a dark mind, nor can your examples of frivolity and light crack these sad, gray oysters. Moreover, why are we so sure a pearl is always inside waiting to be discovered? Some shells are filled with viscous slush, bland souls as salty as the sea but not nearly as alive or as mysterious. Best to let them be.

So I finished sucking the cock of a real beast, a real lip-cracker, a farmer or construction worker, a big man who never looked me in the eye or offered me a casual caress but grunted approval when I maneuvered the meat in my mouth to his liking, evidenced by the enormous quantity of writhing sperm he pumped down my throat. That he left his uncut, softening penis in my mouth was a signal that he expected further service, so I remained on my hands and knees between his legs, one bent, the other outstretched. After what I judged to be a suitable respite, I began to slowly nurse the head just so, the slightest, rhythmic sucking at the pout of his slit, with my tongue supporting the weight of his returning girth. He sighed and extended his other leg, and I knew a second load would eventually spiral down into my stomach. I opened my eyes wide on the off chance that fear was his aphrodisiac, but he had absolutely no regard for me. Rather he was absorbed in watching two men penetrate a much younger, lithe boy who, like me, was made to serve.

The man mastering my mouth absentmindedly fingered his own nipple as my ministrations and the show going on at the other end of the sauna returned him to his own engorged stature. Watery semen, his having been diluted from my previous efforts, began to issue slowly forth, and I gulped and swallowed as he shifted to better rock my face. Even hard, the curtain of his ample foreskin swept my tongue, almost making it a game for me to manipulate and teethe on the head. I then felt the intrusion of another supplicant on his knees pressing up against my side, silently pleading to relieve me of the cock between my lips. This happens all the time. I do not fault the competition, for I have visited many venues where the suckers far outnumbered the men meant to be served. I spat the cock out and he quickly slurped it up in exaggerated gratitude, never once acknowledging me, focusing intently on the meat he so desperately wanted to win over. I squatted there and admired his somewhat hasty style. The brute above us did not deign to take note of this changing of the guards. Soon his second load was unleashed and the groveler at his feet whinnied in pleasure. His devotion was so total, he never once attempted to pleasure himself. As the man we both served disengaged and stepped away, my companion in thirst scooted across the floor in search of more viscous rations, the nub of his penis bouncing against its greasy surface.

As I move from era to era, leaping continents like stones that bridge the stream of time, one thing that frequently changes is the length of foreskin. Some men are shorn, their proud soldiers ready to be served, while others retain their natural glory, like subterranean creatures emerging from their sleep, pushing through folds of flesh to find the mouth that needs them most. Mine.

Another, most welcome discovery: glory holes. Some eras and locations are riddled with these wonders, veritable constellations of teething mouths, red wet puckers desperate to receive. I have been on my knees for such extended periods before one of these openings, eager to entertain any and every piece of meat that slid through the slot, that I was once fearful my legs would fuse. I imagined myself a marooned merman with a pink, useless tail, my body weighed down by a rounded stomach with a pearl-filled primordial soup of semen sloshing within, as I would no longer be able to relieve myself. I tried to shake this dark thought, and I leapt through the next steam room and again the next, until I found a bathhouse with a suitably large swimming pool, the better to exercise my body and rid this image from my mind. So far, this is the only nightmare I have had since Neptune placed his curse upon my lucky brow. And it is one I return to guiltily, again and again, imagining myself swallowing so much cum that it flows out of my mouth until the tiny chamber I am trapped in fills up, and I am afloat for the first time as a wholly aquatic being, in a private fishbowl of regurgitated semen. This mental fantasy always gives me the hiccups.

Back to foreskin. I happened upon a scroll concerning the history of circumcision on one of my rare appearances in a bathhouse in ancient Greece. I devoured every bit of text I could, desperate to absorb as much knowledge between serving some rather pushy and none-too-clean-smelling students as well as an overly entitled but quite hung Roman tax collector. I returned to this book again and again, curious, having been surprised that as I travel through time, foreskin recedes and reappears as if a fleshy but unpredictable tide.

Within this most coveted text, I was shocked to read that the practice had begun with the Egyptian Sun God, Ra. Now the author of the text was a Greek himself, so I approached the work with a healthy amount of skepticism, having been brought up in Rome to believe circumcision was Jewish in origin. The author being Greek, the writings were scurrilously anti-Semitic, though it did give me pause to wonder how the Jewish faith influenced that younger pestilence, Christianity, as the removal of foreskin seemed to coincide with its rise. Of all the religions that bubbled up within the confines of the empire, how much more interesting would the world have become if the Egyptian mythology had taken hold instead of this beleaguered nonsense about Jesus? I would rather have gods with hawk heads than mangy angels with halos any day of the week.

Much later, I found myself in some future Egypt. Upon learning I was in Cairo, I excitedly scoured the premises for a window or access to the roof. I desperately wanted to see if the pyramids still stood. The bathhouse was a cramped affair with a copious amount of cigarette smoke swirling around the low ceiling lights. The men were hushed and anxious to hurriedly connect and quickly leave. I guessed the politics of the time did not allow for any open displays of homosexuality, and thus I could not partake in rooftop sunbathing with vast vistas of buildings and desert and history. Still, I spied a calendar with pictures of the pyramids over the shoulder of a cockeyed youth with a ridiculously high forehead. He was manning the dark hovel where payment was exchanged for towels and a condom. I sighed, wondering how many of Pausanias's Seven Wonders still stood.

❖

Shortly after my visit to Cairo, I was in a dank sauna in New York City. I was sure it was close in era to the Continental. The men had similar wiry and hairy frames, and their fingertips tasted of the same mixture of nicotine and marijuana, but this sauna lacked the festive, charged atmosphere. This was a downtown hunting ground. A dark and lean space, raw wood and chicken wire fencing, cold showers and everyone was on the make, and I was fine with that, so long as they found my mouth an appropriate target.

An impossibly thin man stood in the middle of the breakneck cruising and mouthed words silently. I looked at him and recalled the tutors of my youth. He was speaking to himself in an effort to memorize observations, to piece together a narrative that had hitherto gone unnoticed by the world. He clutched the towel around his taut, wooly stomach as if it were a shield, his compact penis held firm within. He did not want to be touched. He was here to observe. His black, electric eyebrows moved ever so slightly, connoting the swift cursive writing of his mind that his tongue held back. I was a reader witnessing a writer in the very act of composition. I thought to acknowledge this somehow, to let him know that I understood, appreciated, even, that he would soon tell a story that, as far as I knew, had yet to be told.

Men pushed past me, someone cursed, and someone else unseen but close by let out a cry of too urgent release—a veritable shout of ecstasy that gave the more jaded regulars an excuse to laugh dismissively. I spied the author. He caught that laughter and turned it into a wry poem, and I moved on, curious if I would ever stumble upon his book in some other venue at some other time, dog-eared and stained beside a worn leather chair. Would I see him again as an old man, relieved that he finally got it all out? Words on paper, as if that act were somehow both as difficult and as easy as marching into an unknown place in a country you had never before visited, then stripping before others, taking their cocks in your mouth and letting them insert their fingers up your ass for anyone and everyone to see, assess, grade, discuss in class.

CHAPTER SEVENTEEN

No Avail

The lathered warm water stirred as I stilled myself, not yet ready to surface. I had emerged within the aquatic luxury of a massive hot tub. Wizened toes, bland knees, and cocks wavered within like scarlet eels for my choosing.

Needless to say, I can hold my breath for quite a while.

I latched onto the biggest toe to better anchor my bobbing form and blinked away the chlorine and fragmenting filaments of spunk lashing away at my vision. A massive daddy loomed, his beard flowing above, writhing youths at his side, the head of his penis hanging in the manufactured current like a dull ruby red carp lounging in the surf, puckered slit agasp. I minnowed over and lapped at his opening until it extended further, pushing its way into my mouth. I worked the jaw-challenging cock down my throat, an excess of foreskin fanned out across my mouth. Taking him to the root as the waves lapped around my head, I clutched his mass of pubic hair to maintain my position. The hair was a thick, leafy entanglement, an undulating dark emerald that moved like…seaweed.

Fuck.

Fuck Cerberus three times over with a dirty stick in the hottest pit of Hades.

Fuck, fuck, fuckity fuck.

It's my father.

Spitting *his* cock out of my mouth, I somersaulted between his legs and rose, spewing a dramatic fountain of water and pre-cum. And there lounged Neptune in the corner, a punk Ganymede tucked into one armpit, a doleful Hispanic rent boy with a ridiculously large wristwatch nestled in the other. Each offered the god momentary perfection. Neptune's large pink feet bobbed in the water as his massive, ruddy hands cupped the available buttocks. From their moans of pleasure, I could tell Neptune had placed a fingertip within the cleft of their asses and occasionally released slivers of delirious lightning into their systems, resulting in fluttering eyes, chattering teeth, and multiple orgasms, which in turn gave the water an extra dose of froth. The god's white beard, inflated by the swirling waters, roiled across the vast expanse of his chest like a wistful stream. His knees cropped out like craggy boulders. A familiar purple barnacle dully sparkled. I fumed as his penis surfaced, ruefully looking for more prey. He eyed me, and my anger deepened as I realized he did not even recognize his own son. Well, as *one* of his many, many offspring. I should not have felt so dejected. After all, he had only been to my mother's house a few times that I could remember. I had never cared for his drunken philosophizing, the puddles that pooled on the marble floor, filled with the struggling minutiae of sea life his immense being had unmoored, the dank smell he left behind in the kitchen, having devoured whatever seafood the cooks had brought home from the market that day. It was always such a heavy scent, one I now recognized as blood diluted with seawater.

The Hispanic prostitute grinned a sharky grin and licked his thin mustache, momentarily exposing the barest crank of a harelip. He rolled over and presented his moist hole to the god. Neptune's attention drifted over to the proffered ass, and his penis lengthened, splitting his beard into two separate white rivers. His large hands flowed through the water, upending the punk with a splash. Pink mohawk ruined, he struggled to regain his composure. The god mounted the rent boy, who, now far less sure of himself, struggled to catch his breath whenever his head came above water. He sputtered and moaned, and Neptune rode his back as he had ridden whales and underwater mountains, as he had ridden other gods and their mistresses and their mothers, and how, as a young child, eyes wide at the sight of his hanging shaft, I initially formed the idea that he might ride me some day. His ejaculate flooded the hot tub to such a degree that some of his goop was caught in the machinery and all its swirling bubbletry came to a stop. The prostitute was grimly still, floating facedown in the churning waters, as the punk smugly nestled back into Neptune's embrace.

I struggled to speak, to defy him, to renounce his curse as a blessing, but he silenced me with the dismissive wave of a giant hand, flinging water droplets from the emerald webbing between his fingers. A black seahorse bespeckled with its just-spawned young swam within a haze of amber in a ring on his wizened forefinger. Turning to the jaded youth by his side, he relaxed into the water; a scrim of his writhing sperm defined the surface.

"Look, little one, look at all my babies. I have been quite prodigious, that is for sure, but just look at them. Only a few know how to swim in the right direction."

With that, he fixed his gaze upon me. One eyebrow arched, he casually flicked the surface of the water, and wave after wave commenced and the tub was once again aswirl. The resulting whirlpool pulled me downward. The surviving hooker panicked as the wristwatch was sucked from his arm and spiraled down into the unknown. I did not struggle but dove toward the dark center, eager to flee my immortal father and let the salty tide rinse his horrid brine from my mouth. I was flung violently into another bathhouse, in another time, another country. Hong Kong, I believe. A group of lanky boys ignored me as they crowded together to observe a muscled hunk soap himself beneath a cascade of steaming water. The chain of his silver necklace was consumed by perfect pectorals. The heavy lace of his raised armpits elicited soft sighs of appreciation from his naked audience. I stood beside him and took the longest shower. Afterward I worked assiduously to dry myself off in the locker room, going through towel after towel.

To no avail.

❖

I had been to this bathhouse once before. What little I knew of Hong Kong told me it was a large city, crowded, frenetic, stylish—teeming with tourists from all over Asia and parts elsewhere. Though I did not know the name of this establishment, it was such an exquisite oasis I had extended my previous stay. I gathered from overheard conversations that this sauna was renowned for attracting the young and beautiful. They had a discerning door policy that stocked these dark mazes with a myriad of curious, shuffling, naked youths. Towels were hung at the entrance to the basement warren so everyone was on equal footing, that footing shifting across a slick, sticky floor spotted with semen, sweat, and discreetly discarded tissues. I entered the darkened labyrinth. As long as I cruised at just the right speed, I could make occasional contact without rebuffing anyone, and was thus at once on the make and alone with my thoughts.

This journey was meant to willfully release me from family ties, yet the jarring encounter with my father left me shaken. I turned corner after corner of shuffling young men cupping their genitals, edging closer to one another. Newly formed couples ducked into dark alleys. After eons lost in revelry, that the untethered connection with my past could so easily reassert itself…a hand squeezed my buttocks, and I nearly swatted it away. A crush of bodies made passage both difficult and enticing. Instead of indulging, I felt confined and stepped out of the maze.

Beyond the showers, a stairwell led to a dimly lit resting area lined with bunk beds stacked with powder blue vinyl mattresses. Each was occupied by a tanned ephebe, his waist wrapped by a crisp white towel, mesmerized by the ghostly hue of his cell phone, conveniently recharging in the outlet beside each chamber. Certain eras are populated by these hypnotic devices. I am amazed at the power they possess over their supposed owners, who cannot tear away from the lucent screens even when a freshly showered and naked Adonis is making every effort to catch their attention in the locker room.

I lingered here, thinking about how these youths also had to flee their families to become what they were meant to become. What possessed me to think, or even desire, that such an escape would be permanent? This row of splayed boys, some newly arrived, some freshly fucked, all would, at some point, need to go home. So, I guess my discarded struggle, after all these years joyfully adrift, lies in deciding what place I will eventually call mine.

I am unsuited for such despondent thoughts, and when a lissome hand brushed my ankle, I gleefully pivoted. A young jock with crooked teeth leered up at me, his towel tented by the pert stab of his erection. I dove into bed with him. We kissed, lightly at first. His furtive tongue played against my lips as I opened his towel and pulled on his hard cock. I grasped his engorgement while straddling his taut stomach, maneuvering him closer to my opening. He bucked wildly, trying to spear my tight asshole. I pretended to struggle and, failing to grant him entrée, bent backward to lick his tip. He clutched my waist as I successfully positioned myself to lap up his dick, my ass in his face. Boys on either side turned to watch us, eyes moving rapidly from the video games they were playing on their phones to the coupling before them. I slurped on his cock as he licked my slit, orgasm mounting, about to coat my throat—he needed to be home for dinner. I caught him checking the time on his phone while fucking my face. The youths on either side had relinquished their towels and were openly masturbating in unison, a choral whisper of flesh. I was satisfied with the momentary cock in my mouth, knowing I did not need to be anywhere, that wherever I was, it was enough. It was enough.

CHAPTER EIGHTEEN

Final Ceremony

Cocks aside, if not books and scrolls, then music makes me feel complete. That rarity, a live performance, a dance, the rare whirling dervish of towels and paper napkins and everyone is in on the joke, some hilarious drag or the percussionist supreme, naked on drums of overturned buckets and a big bottle. I am the first one to dance. I will dance for the longest time, forever eternally unclothed, and others follow, for I inspire. And perspire. And dive down when the proffered dicks present themselves. Something about the music, and I am *so* there. Which is why I enjoyed the flutist, flawed, exposed, mad, a dancing fool you absolutely would not want to follow, but being near him certainly was enough.

I was happy just to dance and sweat away the sting of that fading familial memory. The flutist was content in his service, perplexed he had so few offers, never understanding what his crotch so obviously offered was an itch and a scratch and a burden, for the poor man was laden with a serious case of crabs. Not just any crabs, but a mythic breed, an immortal irritant, a throbbing pox that you would never be free of once it adhered to your midriff. Countless men sensed this, aghast by the undulation within his ginger pubic jungle. They turned away at his approach. Still, he played on, accompaniment to an otherwise enjoyable orgy.

This sauna had a wondrous maze for cruising and a fantastic dark room. I tasted several men who stood in the doorways of small, rented rooms, and after procuring one myself, I skipped down the hall. The floor was only slightly sticky, and the audible pucker of my bare feet lifting off the viscous surface certified my decision to stick around and really just wallow in place for a bit. I soon wandered into a dark room, delighted to find it a pit of grunting and thrusting, of rolling shoulders, upturned asses and, in general, a shifting feast of wanton men. I forded the fleshy thicket of elbows, knees…and horns. Good ol' Zotikos was rooting around. He snorted as I tapped him on the shoulder, and we both laughed and embraced.

"Watch out for that redhead," he whispered.

"Oh, him? He of a million pinchers!" I finished his sentence.

We giggled and turned our backs to one another, for cocks needed sucking. The bristle of hair hiding his hooves kept tickling my ankles, a nice reminder that some spots were just magical and right. I surrendered to the surrounding men with great abandon, taking any and all offers, the center of attention, my satyr friend and fellow supplicant working hard just to keep up but enjoying my display of sexual prowess.

Much later, I returned to my cabin happily spent and contemplative. The groping, the open mouths, the frenzied throng within these valleys of steam reminded me of the benefits of immortality: if Athena's owl were dedicated to the erotic rather than wisdom (though I had my suspicions that the vocations shared the same wingspan), swooping down into the forge to cut through the fog like a licentious arrow, only to rise again and drift toward other landscapes, over expansive seas. These are night flights, and these sealed, windowless chambers are where fantasies, dark and true, find fruition. That I have visited so many, as either witness or participant, affords me the conviction that these are places where we find our rarer but nonetheless precious truths.

I hung the damp towel on a bent nail, sat on the thin mattress, and inhaled the vivid scents of men: sweat, stale breath, some shit, the diffused fermentations of desperation and fulfillment. The cabin beside was still. Too still. It was too late for Zotikos to have checked out. Earlier, we had established that he would take the cabin next to mine so we could compare notes like two veteran campaigners. No one was wandering the halls. Those who remained did so because they had settled into complicated couplings that would take all night to disentangle, or they were sound asleep, as evidenced by the murmur of snoring that reverberated among the cabins. Or they were gone to the private place only certain drugs unlocked, leaving behind bodies to be used, entered, pissed upon by the malicious or, worse, the bored. Warily I rose, sans tired towel, for this sacred duty was best conducted in the nude. I stepped into the hall, as always amazed at how bronze my skin appeared beneath the pale egg of the suspended light bulb. It was as if I had just stepped off an endless beach and was here primarily to wash the sand from my feet and only chanced upon the opportunity to taste the additional salt of so many men. I sauntered toward my neighbor's cabin and gave the door a knowing knock. There was no answer, so I pushed the door open with two fingers and peered in. Zotikos was on his side, his back to me. He was motionless and seemed to have just exhaled, his next breath taken elsewhere, his shoulders soft, gray spine limp, a knotty cord within a battered bag. I bent over his face and listened for breath. Dry lips parted, a black ooze clung to his swollen, distended tongue.

I stepped out and closed the door, shaking my still-wet locks, both surprised and disturbed at a moment's tumescence between my legs. I moved quickly to the mad flutist's cabin and gave it a hard, swift knock. I heard the man rustle and rise, and with towel in hand, he presented himself. At first, he was perplexed, for he had thought he was being roused as if it was dawn and he was to either vacate or pay for an extended stay. He leaned into the doorframe and leered when he sleepily realized that was not the case. I then pulled the flutist from his cabin by parting his towel and yanking the tip of his limp penis, leading him down the hall by it. The man was baffled, still groggy but eternally hopeful that someone desired him. He stumbled down the hall behind me. I stopped before the satyr's cabin and opened the door with one hand. Excited over the thought of a threesome, the flutist entered and began massaging the old man's shoulder but recoiled at the cold touch. Stricken with fear, he looked at me and then over my shoulder at the door, wild-eyed, craving escape. I stood firm, hands out, and looked the flutist in the eyes. As a godling, I could, in moments of extreme duress or need, give rudimentary commands to mortals, less telepathy or mind control and more a momentary bending of the desire my form naturally demands.

Therefore, I told the flutist what must be done.

The man sighed; obviously he felt misled and trapped, not yet seeing that his brotherly act would release himself from his curse of magical crabs. He sat beside the corpse, weeping, as I settled against the door to see the final ceremony through. The flutist rubbed and massaged the useless crotch of the old man until it possessed some semblance of warmth, and then he lay atop the body and rocked back and forth. The red crustaceans began to migrate from his pubic forest to their new home. They sensed that the body was dead but otherworldly and were eager to burrow into the folds of mythic flesh and wooly, goatish hair. The earnest exodus caused the mad flutist to shake as host shed parasite. He stood over the old man as the last crustacean had left his body. The orange mass moved over the corpse and, instead of settling in the usual dark crannies, began a quiet, orgiastic feast. The flutist tried to flee but I held him, to ensure that every miniature crustacean fled his body, and indeed a few tiny red dots fell to the wooden floor and scurried to join the banquet. The flutist shot me a distraught look, so I let him slip by, and he returned with his musical instrument in hand. We stood there, guarding the door, while he played a somber tune.

Soon the satyr's body was a trembling orange shroud. Occasionally an exposed bone would jut out, but then it, too, would be consumed. One of his chipped and notched horns broke free from the deflating skull and was upended. With a slow swirl, it was devoured as well. The flutist, exhausted, slouched to the floor and fell asleep, his head resting against my vigilant thigh. His shallow breathing masked the last moments of the carapace's consumption. The bloated crabs, black with blood, turned on each other in a scarlet conspiracy of cannibalism. I watched until nothing was left but a dark oil-like substance that stained the planks of the bed frame and dripped between the floorboards. All that remained of Zotikos's essence joined with the bathhouse, adding a dank, underlying scent of primeval forest, a place untrammeled by man, filled with tall trees that shaded proud elk, black moss dripping from their horns.

Absentmindedly petting the head of the sleeping flautist, the image of the satyr's open mouth played repeatedly in my head. The black kiss crusting across his cooling lips, the mark of Obsidio.

CHAPTER NINETEEN

The Last Sound a Drowning Man Hears

So my brother was fording the same shallow waters as me. Was he similarly cursed? I tried to imagine him crossing paths with Neptune—did he bravely challenge the god to try to win my release? Doubtful. It was possible that our worlds merely intersected. The human realm thirsts for death as much as it craves the sensual, both forms of release different sides of the coins Charon collects. Still, I was chilled by the thought that we had occupied the same space and that his actions were deliberate while I was completely unaware.

I walked the halls, scouring every inch of the sauna to see if I could locate Obsidio. The place had pretty much emptied out. A tired-looking man went from cubicle to cubicle flipping mattresses and hustling groggy, hunched men out and toward either the showers and lockers or the booth where they could purchase a ticket for an additional day. A few men showered. Shoulders bunched in the locker room as pants were pulled on, lusterless wedding rings restored. I decided to step into the steam room and let the mist transport me to another time, another place where I could feast and forget, and again take flight, my wings the cocks simultaneously pummeling my mouth and ass until it was as if I were airborne, cruising above mountains of flesh.

❖

I sat on the bench as tendrils of steam slithered across my toes. The whiteness rose from the vents along the floor and soon heat clouded the room, and I felt unmoored. The bench beneath my bare ass receded and, as I had done so many countless times before, I leaned forward as if I were about to dive into the large pool within the Baths of Caracalla. Instead of finding placid waters, I felt a rush as the steam turned into an oceanic tumult. A forceful, swirling tide embraced my body. I am always transported from one place to another within this kind of mystic whirlpool. I feel pressure, the very pressures of time and space, but it is never crushing, just coolly reassuring, and then *voilà*! I am spat out, literally, into another era, having moved across the globe while traversing time in what feels like mere seconds.

The sting of salt water has never bothered me, considering my progenitor, so for the first several eons of voyaging, I peered long and hard into the waves rocketing my body, to see if I could determine their source. Perhaps a gigantic kraken spewed forth this private water spout, and I could crawl backward across his massive tongue and toward the origin to discover…what, exactly? This was not a carnival ride I necessarily wanted to end. Still, I struggled to keep my eyes open against the onslaught, and I never saw the source of the whirlpool that claimed my body and flung it here and there around the world. If I were tunneling through the ocean, surely I would see the bows of boats, a tangle of seaweed or darting fish. Only once did I see something unusual.

Exiting a memorable night at a Spanish bathhouse—oh,

how their mouths have chewed the calculus of Latin into something syrupy, seductive, and when I was on my knees, sweetly demanding—I launched into my dive and immediately noticed a glimmer just over my shoulder. I twisted as a swimmer gulping for air to see the trailing glow of a large luminescent jellyfish. I blinked to make sure none of the poppers I had just huffed were clouding my brain. When I opened my eyes, it was still drawing closer, with a quickening pulse of light illuminating every exciting dimple of its calmly undulating form. Caught within its gelatinous body, a perfectly intact human skull rode a jelly throne through a funnel in time. Just as I reached out to make contact with this peaceful messenger, the water rushed and, in a mad swirl, I was deposited on the floor of a crowded steam room. I was surrounded by the dark shadows of men, one who turned and, seeing me on my knees, pointed his penis and doused me with urine as if I were a fire he needed to put out.

I traveled repeatedly, desperate to put as much distance between the unwelcome family reunions and myself. There were so many days-nights-mornings-evenings, freed of even the awareness of time it was hard to imagine a life measured, opposite this secret and separate Sargasso Sea within which I float. Oh, the stories I have picked up from sailors. How I have loved the ones I was able to taste before they showered or bathed—that seasoned oil of labor, sweat, the salt of battering waves. I imagined, several times over, that whichever bathhouse I currently occupied was in actuality a sunken ship, an overturned ark of sighs, forgotten on the ocean floor, stocked with moribund, starving sailors sucking sustenance from each other. By working my mouth and ass, with my body spread like a sheet to catch the wind, I would be able to lift this doomed ship. For that is what it felt like, some nights. The sauna full, brimming with erotic energy, yet an aura of loneliness hovering over the hot proceedings, forcing us to cling that much more to one another, as if we could all fill the hollow spaces with sweat and breath. Whenever this feeling descended upon me, I knew it was time to travel.

❖

Ready to depart again, I stepped into the deep end of a most azure pool of wintry water, and colorless bubbles rose around me, weaving wreaths of frolicking impermanence. Sinking downward, the bubbles coalesced into the white petals of an aqueous plant, one meant to shoot seed through the darker caverns of human interaction. I thought, well, if I am the spore, why not try to assert my direction? And so, again instinctively assuming the arc of a diver, I waited until I was subsumed by the watery charge and I shot upward, attempting to alter my course. I pushed toward my left and felt my form rock back and forth, as if in a swing made of waves, and the water slapped my face as if in reprisal of my anarchistic efforts. The force spread my lips, and the salty froth scoured my gums until I thought they might bleed.

This sparked the odd erotic memory: a rotund chef in a bathhouse in Nice flipped me over and nudged his fat sausage toward my crack. When I resisted, he drunkenly snorted, "blood is nature's lubricant," before stuffing his meat up my unready hole. This was in the back room, no lights save a fluorescent pink sign that screamed "SORTIE" that painted the men stalking the circular hallway surrounding the black bunker a craven hue. The dark den within was a scene of some of the most relentless fucking I had ever endured or witnessed. It was a room of total surrender. I was pummeled by a train of cock, every member whetted from the previous bleeding ass or spittle or sweat or from similar, effusive cornucopias of cum just as my righteous hole had become. I was but one among the throng on the floor, elbows blackened by the flakes of ancient semen and shit that tiled the ground beneath a multitude of bent and broken beasts. But how I digress.

I plunged rather than rode, for the first time directing my body. The forces that carried me buckled and pitched in retaliation. Fear filled me. Could I, the son of Neptune, drown? That darker, colder, invisible hand of the ocean gripped my throat, and I remembered as a child rolling in the waves off our seaside villa, realizing the tinkle of the shells and tumbling coral I heard underwater would be the last sound a drowning man hears.

And I emerged, born again into the world of men who feast on other men. I plopped down hard on a familiar bench. The bathhouse in Spain. The towel on the floor was just as I had left it, but not that dead man in the corner. He was alive when I was last here, which, judging from the familiarity of the room, its warmth, the smells in the air, was only moments ago. I searched the sauna. Everyone was dead. Men lay on the floor of the changing room, lockers open. A man floated in the shallow cooling pool, his wrists bobbing as if he had just been released from the cruelty of the crucifix. I examined a body slumped against the door of the dry sauna, towel discarded by his fall, the question mark of his flaccid cock now forever unanswered in a nest of riled, straw-like pubic hair. He was so beautiful, not quite young, one of those older men who hold on to their looks as if their very appearance were their true foundation, and not the bones and muscle that propped it all up. I hoisted his head up by the chin. Black ooze dribbled out of his slack mouth. I fell backward in disbelief of what I had already sensed to be true: Obsidio had slain these men.

My heart tried to leap out of my sallow chest. I looked over my shoulder as if my demonic brother might be behind me, but this was a quiet place, a still place, as still as a charnel house after the gravediggers depart. I went momentarily mad with speculation. *How did he follow me? How did he sow such destruction?* I thought of our trip to Athens, the pod of porpoises that rode our ship's wake and, recognizing me as a son of Neptune, frolicked in the waves, winking at me in spirited delight. *He* was riding my wake. Whenever I departed a place, he was able to step into the vacuum my traveling form made before the watery forces closed in on itself. *How many steamy utopias, what rare erotic playgrounds has he destroyed? And then how did he find me again?* Zotikos's slaying was not some mere coincidence. At some point, our paths must have crossed. Eons ago, he stood in the shadows and watched how my curse played out in reverse, delighting me and a multitude of others. He must have realized that this, too, was a buffet for the true gourmand, and that he could not only join in but spoil it, to his immense satisfaction. As I fed on life, so he gorged on death. But at that moment, I doubted his powers were as they are now. His mischief so vile and far-reaching. No, it was when he found me a second or third time that he hatched such a plot. And why not? I was the one body he could claim whose soul he could not snuff out. How maddening, to be the personification of death and not be able to own that which you desired most. So he would torment me until he could claim me as his sole property again. No matter where I went, he could follow and punish all whom I had provided succor. How could I resist? Stop my travels and stay in one place, imprison myself in an abandoned bathhouse for all time. Then I would never know if he was satisfied with my self-imposed banishment. What was there to stop him from continuing this roving holocaust? He *is* the personification of death. He has all the time in the world.

However, I knew of one such temple he would never willingly visit, a place he would never think to look, as it was in his backyard, so to speak.

CHAPTER TWENTY

Mouths Agape

There are, indeed, myths known only to the mythmakers. Once I had become aware of Obsidio's sinister powers, I researched his father, Pluto, within the luxurious libraries of the Baths of Caracalla, to better comprehend the bloodline and see if some action or unction could undo the deadly intent of his seed. The often-told story of Persephone, Queen of the Underworld, had permutations, iterations, in poems and bald prose retellings. I uncovered no useful knowledge in my hellish research, though through deeper investigations in ancient texts, I was able to discover that the landscape of Hades was far more complex than I had imagined. There were entire cities filled with shades, some quite similar to those within the empire. Many, however, were not. No, it was via a tale told by quite a different "queen" that I learned the underworld possessed its very own bathhouse.

An unnamed Bithynian poet, a dedicated lover of boys whose work is far from lost but was rather decidedly erased from literary history by the church, recorded a brief description of just such a place. He referenced other equally vanished works about a haven for deceased sodomites and their ilk, implying an epic of Homeric proportions had once existed detailing the exploits of the residents who haunted this murky palace. Though I failed to find a method to dam the darkness issuing forth from my brother's throbbing member, the image of this place in Hades never faded from memory. Now that I had tentatively learned to navigate the watery gates of my travels, I took aim, diving deep, heading downward like never before. Best I escape to hell, where all the souls had already had the life force Obsidio craved wrung out of them, I thought. Surely I would be safe among the shades.

Even though I did not require oxygen, the pressure and increasing darkness of my plunge filled me with fear. I nearly reversed course as the waters took on all the blackness of the void and the temperature dropped to the point where my clenched teeth chattered mightily. I lost all sensation in my hands as I tried to ford this invisible stream toward hell. Then suddenly the temperature stabilized, and I found myself headed upward toward faint light. Breaking through the surface, I sputtered and gasped, afloat in Hades.

I was alone in a large pool, the water tepid and thick, more like spittle than anything deposited from an aqueduct. The sky above was cracked and earthen, the distant roof of a massive cave. The source of light was invisible and as prevalent as it was diffused, with enough illumination to see but not understand. I rolled into a backstroke, eager to explore my new hideaway. Mounting the steps out of the pool, I had to push through a lumbering mass of shades. These ghosts were mute, shambling things. Eyeless, mouths agape, they clawed and groped one another with fruitless abandon. Unfulfilled hunger was their only form. Whenever a shade attempted sexual congress with another, their ghost cocks would become as ethereal as twisting fog, only to reappear once they moved on in frustration. I pushed my way through the swarming horde, looking for a spot of respite. The marble beneath my feet was cracked and crumbling. Black vine strangled the familiar columns surrounding the pool. As I made my way down a recognizable hall, I realized this subterranean bathhouse was a replica of none other than the Baths of Caracalla. I could return to the library and study in peace. Centuries of books and scrolls awaited. I just had to fight through this thicket of ghouls.

Gray, transparent hands pawed my thighs and backside. The pressure of countless dead souls was suffocating, but I moved on, relieved to find the familiar library relatively free of shades. A lone dead philosopher kept tripping over his tattered toga while attempting to reach a once-coveted scroll. I thought to assist but worried that if this was his fate, I could somehow inherit it, or something worse and unimaginable would happen if I intervened.

My favorite seat near a tall window was available. I touched the familiar blue, tasseled cushion, and it turned to dust. No matter. Once I was lost in a familiar ode, no amount of discomfort would distract. I scanned the shelves for something demanding and longish, thinking to bury myself in texts for millennia. All of the authors I had yet to devour would divert me from the monster sibling rampaging across the living world. His hunger for breathing souls would keep him from ever finding me here, ensconced among the dull departed. I pulled down a fat scroll, the first book of Livy's opus. I had long avoided the history of the republic, so noble and exemplary, preferring the feverish poetics of gods and monsters, or contemporary gossip, tales of imperial treachery and debauchery; but reading good old Livy would be like slipping into the icy waters of a vast *frigidarium,* a tonic to the fraught adventures I had endured of late. Settling into my spot by the window, I unrolled the scroll and gazed upon a white nothingness. The parchment was empty. I blinked and thought this a prank or some odd mistake, but upon reviewing the nearest tome, I realized this emptiness was replicated throughout the library. All of the pages of every document were blank.

Of course. This made perfect sense. After all, what lessons can you learn once you are dead?

❖

The bathhouse of Hades revealed itself to be much, much larger than the Baths of Caracalla, which, as a faded replica, was but a facet within seemingly endless labyrinths. This immense composite of a multitude of bathhouses from across the empire and time, some real and some imagined, stretched across the topography of Hell. A stairwell led down to what must have been private imperial chambers reserved for water sports far different from what the rabble observed when the Coliseum was flooded and gladiators took to fighting one another on miniature ships. The shade of an emperor, his gray visage tinged with purple, was on his knees, permanently parched as he turned from ghostly slave to ghostly slave, their flickering erections ever dissipating when the shreds of his lips strained for contact. The surrounding men all appeared to be relieving themselves upon his haunted form in equally thwarted revenge. The wisps of urine that streamed from their white cocks dissolved before reaching his black open maw. Other rooms were thick with shades rubbing up against each other, but without any erotic friction. And the pools, whether meant to be warm or cold, all felt an unsatisfactory tepid temperature, the same as the stale air that filtered through the statue-filled halls, statues of familiar forms I somehow could not place. Forlorn, I decided to retrace my steps back to the Baths of Caracalla. Possibly the sacred spot beneath the caldarium, where the Fellatiolympics were held, retained some hot spark of life.

❖

As I navigated a length of marble stairs, the press of shades was so concentrated I could barely make progress. I pushed hard against the jellied shoulders of multiple spirits. Their ectoplasmic forms seemed concocted of cold slush, though I tried to avoid sustained contact; their touch was repulsive to the living such as I. *Would I remain living if I stayed here too long?* I knew enough not to eat or drink while in Hades—even a nibble or sip guaranteed permanent tenancy. But what about simply staying past one's welcome? I had half a thought to head back to the library and read up again on all the devious traps and pitfalls a visit to hell entails, before I remembered that all the books were uniformly bare.

I forded this packed tributary of the departed and discovered this otherworldly version of the basement was quite different from the one I experienced. I faced an infinite hall of glory holes. Shade after shade pulled at their brothers who were positioned on their knees before each opening, desperately trying to pry them away and take their place. As a corporeal being, I was able to exert myself and push past them, the better to see what spirit-penises summoned such a conflagration from the other side of the glory holes. No cold cock waited. I peered through one such opening and looked out across an immense, pallid moat, an undulating river of slowly percolated sperm. This endless tributary of rolling opalescence spread in every direction. Gray tongues hung from an infinite row of small openings, glory holes forever out of reach from the slow slap of sticky waves that beat soundlessly against the marble walls of the bathhouse of Hades. *A looping river of cum. But how deep? What source?* As deep as any and every untapped desire. The source was every erotic dream deferred, every dream dreamed since men stopped being dumb animals and grew into the self-appointed guardians of one another's needs and intentions. Regret begets just such a White Nile, and how the unquenched are hung out to dry, like desiccated crocodiles, all teeth and tongue, scales like jewels that could not buy you more than a passing, judgmental smile.

The men haunting this never-ending stretch of glory holes are not the forbearers of the vices on display; rather, these poor souls belonged to those who never once partook. They are the denied. The hesitant. Those hungry men who never tasted other men. The men who thought a "sin" imagined was somehow worse than one committed, not knowing that "sin" is defined as much by inaction as anything else. Their name is Legion.

This was not my intended brotherhood. At least not yet. As I was alive, my presence among the living was required. I rushed up the stairs and parted the spectral throng. Back at the Baths of Caracalla simulation, I took a running leap and dove into the lukewarm pool.

❖

Colorless steam hissed and billowed as I sat, shaking off the pull of the vortex, desperate to get warm yet left cold from all that I had discovered. I was in a familiar, albeit nondescript, bathhouse. One that Obsidio had yet to touch. Someone let out a hopeful cough, more to announce their presence than clear their ready and willing throat. I moved away. I tried to gather my thoughts, but fear and confusion ran a chariot race inside my empty skull, kicking up clods of grit, the crumbly stuff my brain used to consist of.

After I dove into the water, I looked down and saw what Obsidio must have discovered one hellish morning, taking a constitutional swim: my travels had left open what I can only describe as otherworldly tidal pools. Floating there, I could see my footprints across the earth, mirrored reflections of every place that I had ever been. Open portals. All he had to do was dip in, and there he would be, appearing almost immediately after I had departed.

I wanted to tally the dead. To lovingly bury the corpses so many families would disown once the bodies were discovered in such ill-reputed establishments. Unknowingly, I had created one battlefield after another, my tracks across time a march toward certain doom for those I left behind.

I alone could stop this madness. I needed to find my brother and rein him in, capitulate in every way, cry to Mount Olympus for Father to rescind my curse and allow me to wallow in the dry pits of Hades, a poor beast tethered to my brother's ankle, loping beside him like a hellhound, lapping at his long, deadly dick wherever and whenever he stopped to inspect some novel torture device or question a newly arrived shade.

I did not even have to go and find him. I just needed to be somewhere where he could find me. The stream grew thicker, and I leaned in, ready to dive into the cold, deadly pool of fate.

CHAPTER TWENTY-ONE

Hades's Swimming Pool

The rooms were all dark. Even with the lights on, darkness was as pervasive as an insipid fog, for his deadly touch had emptied out untold erotic palaces. I walked once-familiar halls and heard no sounds, saw no other men. Some of these places had been shuttered so quickly that moldering towels still clung to wet floors. Others had been stripped until they were unrecognizable and denuded spaces save the unmistakable odor of chlorine. And death. My brother's slipstream of carnage was a meandering path of unreal cruelty made more painful in that he was following my dainty wet footsteps across the tiled floors of what should have been an adventure for any and all. These sanctuaries were not supposed to conceal a death sentence. And not one delivered during such intimate, naked moments of touch and sharing, making executioners out of kiss and cock.

As I dipped into the hellmouths at the bottom of Hades's swimming pool, I found scenes of cruel murder and obscene catastrophe. Naked bodies on steam room floors kept warm by the heated environs, black semen seeping out of cold cavities. The limp body of a blond ephebe in a sling suspended from the ceiling, the men lined up to fuck him unaware that he had expired, not surrendered. An entwined couple on a black vinyl mattress as still as the statues of fallen Grecian warriors beneath the flickering thrusts of pornographic films playing in a continuous loop on screens embedded within slick walls. Mouths slack with cooling drool against glory hole cavities as lifeless as open graves. Room after room revealed the ransacked churches of my secret pagan fraternity. These rare spaces of sexual reprieve—for some, living during eras of oppression or at the very least circumspect times, their only literal succor—now desecrated. Now destroyed.

Once I realized certain tidal pools opened into vistas wherein he had decimated the populace, I forced myself to return. I needed to take census of the butchery for my anger to build, to fuel the strength I would need to take down Obsidio and avenge my true brothers.

I arrived within a small, homey bathhouse in San Francisco, thick with incense and laughter. I had not been to this one often and had assumed its existence was short-lived, but I always enjoyed its bohemianism, the casual mixture of drugs and sex. The men smelled more like men here and were far less preened and plucked than in other time periods. Now it was a lifeless husk. A body lay half in and half out of a small cabin. A twist of sheets covered the face and torso, revealing young legs and a shrunken cock encased in a sticky cocoon of its own semen, the last expulsion of life.

I parted more drapes of mist and steam. A familiar bathhouse in Berlin. Men fully clothed in uniforms towered above nude corpses talked into black radios strapped to their shoulders. I hid behind a cart brimming with dirty towels and observed the dismissive way they regarded the dead, as if the men on the floor were simple bags of trash. They smoked cigarettes and brusquely joked under their breath. Some of the cruder men even took pictures of the bodies, arranging them in ridiculous postures. Their colleagues chortled. One young ambulance driver stiffened as he entered the locker room. I sensed he was a regular patron and that his assumed indifference to the scene of carnage was a gross act. His coworkers did not know about his love for other men. He rolled a body onto a gurney and pretended to smirk as one of the policemen helped push the carcass with the heel of his boot. I understood that reflexive fear kept him from crying, from attacking these beasts, but as the color drained from his cheeks, I also knew today's horror would turn to tomorrow's shame. This inaction would haunt him long after the perpetrators had forgotten their weak humor in the face of tragedy.

The next sauna was again a gruesome sight: small, cramped, dank and hot. The bodies had gone undiscovered for too many days. Lifeless flesh had erupted into malodorous cankers. Unregulated heat had quickened decomposition. Gray flesh slid off blunt steeples of bone. Sickened and saddened, I stumbled across the killing field, my hand over my mouth to stifle the dry heaves racking my upper body. I pushed through a filmy curtain to what I hoped was the shower room so I could flee this mad panorama of death. In the darkness, I brushed against another body and recoiled as he howled to life. I was relieved to find someone alive, but his howl hollowed out as he fell to the ground and pushed away from me across the floor in wild desperation. His arms outstretched to ward me off, I could see his fingernails were long and his hair unkempt. This naked, hungry man had been trapped among the dead. I could only imagine how he survived Pluto's Kiss, as the devastation had been named in those locations that somehow remained open after a visit from Obsidio. Perhaps he was napping in a dark corner of the steam room. Possibly he was one of those birdlike voyeurs who visit the baths, standing in the corner for hours, observing the various couplings, ranking the bodies but never touching any of them. How he looked at me, eyes wide with terror, silently begging that I not come any closer; he thought *I* was the demon that had delivered death. I saw him as the penultimate harbinger for my true mission. I must keep this from happening again.

❖

During my travels, I had visited specific palaces of exquisite vice only once, while others I had returned to again and again, across the eons, very little changing among the interlocking bodies, the lust-filled basements and large subterranean pools. I understood the vagaries of such establishments and that the changing morals and even laws of certain cultures and countries naturally led to the closings of these businesses. But now also this ebony drip of plague. I was not responsible for the initial onslaught of this fraternal pestilence, but I soon would be if I did not do everything in my power to put a stop to the next sexual slaughter.

Chapter Twenty-Two

And So I Brought Him Home

I had been in the bathhouse for only a few minutes before I realized by the language, the playfulness of the men, that I had landed in one my favorite bathhouses in Montreal. I always enjoyed the men here, the earthy locals, the eager and interesting tourists. A jovial atmosphere filled the place.

I exited the sauna and entered a large, subterranean room with a swimming pool. Men lounged about in the nude, assessing one another or lost in thought, taking a break from all the revelry going on in the other chambers above. I felt the temperature in the air subtly drop.

My brother and your death rose from the waters like a black dolphin. Unlike me, he had aged since our last meeting. Taller, he somehow appeared to be trying to hide his height by bringing his shoulders in, as if he wanted to conceal his dark powers. He looked at me and smiled a toothless smile; the smoldering amusement he exhibited was infuriating. My cheeks burned as he caught my eye and gestured lewdly down toward his pelvis with a sweep of long, mantis-like fingers. His penis had lengthened since I had seen him last. It hung between his sleek, muscled thighs like a midnight eel, charged with electric menace. My knees buckled slightly, as I wanted it inside me again, filling my mouth with its balanced fury. I worked my jaw in anticipation as he stood there, waiting for me to return to my rightful and only real vocation. Oblivious, men on either side of the pool involuntarily shivered and slid down farther into the water, as if the chill were in the air and not standing before them. The shimmering net of blue tiles at their backs caught the reflection of a thousand minnows of light, throwing them across the curved ceiling above. A slight mist rose, obscuring Obsidio's cock and his brief ebony bush. His skin had darkened, as if he had spent his days committed to some outside sport and not within ruptured tombs or exacting ceremonies in broken and abandoned churches, shifting across time and space the way a shark calmly cuts cold channels. I leaned in and tried to part the ferns of mist with my eyes.

There it was. Every contour I remembered was calling to me, that heavy, almost droopy head, the beautiful flange of flesh. His coil of foreskin receded slightly, and the redness of his head shone through like the tip of a giant viper's tongue, an angry beacon of lust. It pulled me forward. My mouth felt dry, and I swallowed a nearly forgotten hollowness, an added dimension of raw need: my original thirst. I was possessed by a personal knowledge of gravity as I stepped into the pool, shocked at how cold the water had become. I knelt before him as a supplicant bending before his most worthy king and extended my tongue as if in handshake, welcoming a long-absent ruler back into his castle's throne. I suddenly recalled that time in the cemetery, as I lay across the body of a dead boy. The dirt in the corner of his placid eye. Obsidio had lured me there not only to fuck me, but to see if I would survive his seed. Nothing more than a cool experiment. Certainly nothing less.

And so I brought him back home. Into my mouth. The place where his passions were born and nurtured.

We joined and I sought eternity, a timeless period where I housed his lust inside me, breathing and massaging his dark cock with my tongue as it filled my throat, my emptiness. The very curse placed upon me by my father Neptune wavered. The joy I felt threatened to rend the universe itself apart, I so violated the concept of punishment this existence was supposed to visit upon my servile frame. I craved Obsidio's pungent, heavy spunk. It was so thickly seeded that I often thought of masticated, rotting grapes as I gulped his semen down—not that I did not want to savor it, but I needed to move it quickly into my stomach so I could be better prepared for the next lumpy load.

The dark sediment that had caught on the ridges of his shaft came loose in my mouth. I was able to massage them into smaller particles between my tongue and his penis. My taste buds discerned the effluvia of black deeds and dried semen, specks of shit, and the metallic tinge of blood. I swallowed the dissipating granules while making the mental note to try and be more observant when I next excreted my pearls in a few months. Perhaps some of this current grit would add a touch of color, punctuating the milky quartz with a starry rise, or even transform one of the jewels into something like a cat's eye, staring up at me in malignant judgment as I fished it out of the toilet.

As I sucked my brother's dick, I wondered how many souls had knelt before him, serving him so tenderly and with such admirable surrender as to warrant something kinder than an actual kiss of death.

I clutched his calves and was disappointed that they had substantially changed shape in my absence. As Obsidio had grown, his leg muscles had elongated. Gone were the grooves and veins I used to steady myself. The back of his legs used to be as recognizable as a favorite discus to the thrower, but he had changed, and this unfamiliar canvas mesmerized me.

That death actually stalked the halls of sodomy—oh, how *that* would titillate some sour Christians. This schizophrenic sect, that incestuous threesome, how they have harried my fellow catamites since long after Rome tried and failed to stamp their pestilence out. Ironically, they survived and unknowingly made Obsidio a central figure in their mad myths. I had seen his visage countless times before and had failed to recognize him tattooed on arms and chests of men traipsing the halls eon after eon. He is their devil. Rumor and exaggeration had turned his dark complexion into a vivid red hue. They assigned him horns to better illustrate his satyrlike lust. Legend lengthened his already considerable penis into a whiplike tail. I ran my fingers down to his sharp heel bone and breezily lingered there, a maneuver which always drove him mad with delight.

I heard the familiar, appreciative sigh, which was as close to a thank you as I had ever received all those years ago. *How many years?* Drunk on some peculiar ambrosia, I had once driven myself to distraction trying to count backward and tally all the times my tongue had tasted from this ongoing cornucopia of cocks, where and how often my ass was entered. However, in my obsessive delirium, I hit about the idea that really, this was not an adventure, and most definitely not the curse as it was intended to be. This was an ocean. I was joyously lost at sea. As if to bear the point home, Obsidio let loose a torrent of urine down my throat. It must have been ages since he had taken a piss, so much hot brine flooded my internal channels. I steadied myself against the gulping onslaught, and with a mental gasp of delight, I recalled a line from Lucretius, "For thee the Ocean smiles." Now, though, I realized this ocean began and ended with my brother's cock in my mouth.

❖

Obsidio showered. I waited with a fresh towel across my outstretched arm. I needed to be his slave. Rather, I needed him to enslave me. He would have nothing but disdain toward voluntary service. However, if I pretended to flee and was accidentally successful, or if his interest in me was only fleeting at best, then his lust would again be genocidal. As he turned under the water, I caught sight of his perfect penis and almost dropped the towel. This he witnessed from the corner of his eye and was quietly pleased. I would not have to grovel, then. He had taken note that my natural sense of servitude had recommenced. Fine. Let him claim me as a pet so all would be right in the world. I will drink his darkness so that all may live.

Greedily so.

CHAPTER TWENTY-THREE

Pluto's Kiss

After his shower (cold, of course), I blindly followed him around the bathhouse. He was like a predator, noting all of the dark corners, assessing where men gathered. I licked my lips, ready to feast on his length, to please him utterly, though he had gained a snake's swiftness and for a moment I lost him in the locker room. As I turned the corner, Obsidio kissed a man. He held his head in his hands, one finger coated in wet shadow. He touched that finger to the man's lips playfully, as if asking him to keep a secret.

As the surprised corpse slipped to the floor, Obsidio caught the swinging locker door in his hand, pulled out a pair of neatly folded black jeans, and shimmied them on. I reflexively knelt to help the man, as if what oceanic powers I possessed could reverse my brother's deadly touch. But I, of course, could not. The sea is a conduit of life, not life itself, and Obsidio had become more than the visage of death, he *was* death. I had not yet observed up close the gross nonchalance with which he took life, and my stomach guttered like a candle. I rose and clenched my fists as if to strike him, but he had sped past the other dressers, their actions slowed, mouths agape, as their brother slumped down on the floor. He turned and laughed as the exit door slowly swung closed behind him.

Enraged, I left the dead man and marched toward a water fountain crammed between a soda machine and an old coin-operated condom dispenser that also sold aspirin and Alka-Seltzer and mouthwash. I grabbed one of the conical paper cups and went over to the hot tub. An old man arched an eyebrow as I dipped the cup in the water and filled it up to the paper rim. I turned toward the door but paused. I had never ventured outside like this before. Sure, I had mounted a balcony, lain on a rooftop tanning deck, testing the boundaries of my god-placed spell, but nothing as overt as the action I was about to take. I pushed through the crowd that had gathered and stepped over the body of the dead man. As I pulled his shirt out of the still-open locker, a twink with an absurdly overdeveloped upper body glared at me as if I had come to rob a corpse rather than save my brotherhood. I looped one arm through the sleeve of the button-down and switched hands to squirm into the other, all while trying not to slosh the cup of water. As weary paramedics kicked open the door, I slipped past.

Montreal was in full revelry while I was in a private storm. A dark churn of reality, as if gravity itself were slamming against my still-boyish body with a lash of knife-sharp, invisible wind. A vicious undertow gripped me and tried to pull me back toward the bathhouse. I soldiered on as if I were walking beneath the sea, the sand under my feet quick and slippery. I kept as many of my fingers in the cup of water as possible without displacing too much of the precious fluid. Men and women packed the streets, also cupping their drinks, but with cheer and laughter. I held on to mine the way a sea captain holds the mast as his ship is heaved back and forth. The lights, the night air, air! Unfiltered by steam, cramped quarters, and sweaty bodies, the luxurious silk of fresh air ran beneath my nostrils. This distraction caused me to momentarily lift my fingers from out of the cup, and I felt the full force of the tidal current swirl at my back. The pull was unbelievably strong, but I shook my head and caught a whiff of Obsidio. His rich, mammalian smell, which I had always associated with the dirt a strigil would scrape off a goat, caught beneath the ample hood of his foreskin; the scent, which I had found so alluring in my distant youth, well, I knew now its true and deadly origin: sweet carrion. I nearly retched as I pivoted and homed in on my prey.

Death was inside a strip club. Surely all the boys were dancing for him, whether they knew it or not.

The doorman gave me a puzzled look and was about to physically position himself between me and the entrance when I caught his eye and used every ounce of my celestial charm to sway him. He blinked, I glowed, he wavered, and I passed. My first impression was that I had entered a sparkling bordello. The boy leaving the stage possessed the look of a professional wanton, and the pale meat hanging between his legs, though impressive, had the wrung-out quality of a well-used washcloth. His eyes were distant and calculating.

Not so the pixie who bounded onto the stage as his fellow stripper stepped down to seduce a few more dollar bills from the assorted drunks and tourists in the audience. All of them sat, mouths gaping, aglow in the same golden amber of small table lamps, uniting them in a drunken, lustful hue. This young man took the stage as if it were life itself and he its gleeful conqueror, his proud penis not only fully erect but bouncing off his beautiful stomach, a slight youthful paunch, as a silver-sticky-singular web of pre-cum bobbed between tip and belly button. He smiled and looked at me, then pivoted to acknowledge every member of the audience not currently digging into the proffered crotch of his colleague. Then with an athletic flourish of his hand, he again drew attention to his moist, hard cock, as if we needed to be reminded of why we had all gathered here. Well, I did not. My goal was to keep him alive, and the generations of boys yet to be born that did not deserve Pluto's Kiss.

Syncopated music and lights filled the room with throbbing geometric patterns. He swiveled his lithe hips, cock twirling, and I thought to lean in close and catch a stray flying teardrop of semen in my mouth, to quench my thirst as I scanned the room for my brother, but then I caught sight of him. The tired stripper who came before the gyrating Ganymede mechanically turned his back to the audience and parted a red curtain. As the flap closed, I could see the men's room. Obsidio stood before a urinal, his wolf's penis extended, about to let loose a torrent within the cracked porcelain basin.

I entered the bathroom, and he let fly a rueful laugh.

"Look at that, a fish walking on land. Lucretius was right, all life began in the sea!"

He turned, and as he did so, the jeans he had stolen dropped to his ankles. He displayed his lethal cock, knowing it would cast a spell over me. I had already transgressed the boundaries of my curse more than I thought possible. My knees quivered at the sight of it. His penis was as hypnotic as always, the perfect, flaring head, the reptilian folds beneath, and the extensive length, serpentine, spotted like a snake that lived in a volcanic basin.

I dropped my preserving cup of water as Obsidio again unleashed a torrent of urine on my face. This golden salt water cemented me to the floor, to this room, in this moment. I was free to service him, so I gulped and swallowed while placing my hands between his ass checks, the hair there coarse like a donkey's—black as a midnight charnel pit. I combed it with my fingers, untangling hard knots fused by the charcoal of shit and the grime kicked up from horseback rides through Hades. The head of his penis pushed through my lips, and I kissed it. I tongued the brine still brimming in his slit as he sighed, gripping my hair like the red hell-stallions he tamed under his father's tutelage. Piss dripped off my chin as more of his length filled my throat. I welcomed the sacrament of this familiar and familial girth. As I did so, I felt sorry for him He was doing all that his father had bred into him. Not I. I was the rebel who reveled, who flaunted desire. His killings were not born of any need. I was wrong to think he murdered for sport. His was a hunger as unbridled as mine. However, where he was purposeful, I was gloriously lost in a shadowy aquatic forest filled with bizarre coral castles and beckoning mermen. I was at play. He, at work. His cravings had become a scythe I must still. Tears crept into the corners of my eyes as my tongue snaked around his column of flesh and milked from it what I needed. Sure enough, his dark seed issued forth, with all the dank weight of dirt on a fresh grave, and I gulped while maintaining the bulk of the black pulp spackled across my tongue. Another gush of hot urine followed, and I pretended to wash his effluvia from my face with this providential shower. He was spent. As his shoulders slumped, I rose and thumbed one of his nipples tenderly, lovingly—as playfully as when we first started to couple. He grinned, and I looked at him wide-eyed and tilted my head, and he instinctively leaned in for a kiss. I embraced him hard, with arms that would not let go. My tongue pried open his cracked, raw lips, which relented more from surprise than my strength. I slathered the cavern of his mouth with the seminal death he had painted on so many other faces, across so many beautiful lips, some so young that they had yet to fully sing the song that was their soul. Like them, he was not immune, as I was, to his own poisonous kiss.

I would like to think the look he gave me as he clutched his throat and began to jerk and writhe was one of knowing release, but it was not. It was the real anger of a carnivorous beast, angry not that it was dying but that dying meant it would not feed on the flesh of others again. So he collapsed and I felt my form waver, as it did in the clouds of steam. His body shook and turned to ribbons of red flesh that in turn tore at each other until all that was left was a dissipating mass. I started to sweat. No, it was not sweat but drops from the ocean, a crashing wave I couldn't see coming to transport me to another place, another time.

It was far past time for me to go.

A black speck shambled out from the middle of the thick pink primordial part of the undulating accumulation that had been my brother. It was a beetle, black as the pupils of Obsidio's ambitious eyes. I thought to stomp it before I was taken from this place and even raised my foot but imagined that in my absence the goo of the crushed insect would revolt into a thousand teeming maggots ready to reform an entirely new and unknown carapace of death.

I scooped up the bug and popped it my mouth.

Better to consume death itself than be consumed in turn by imaginary unknowns.

Then I was gone.

CODA

This time it felt like I was walking in the rain. All of my other movements, parting the curtains of steam or plunging through tidal forces, I had been pressed from one reality to the next, but now I was walking, hands out as always, pulling aside sheets of water without the pressure of *time*.

I continued, not yet entering another room or bathhouse. It had been centuries since I had gone for a walk. It felt like a luxury. I looked down at the gray, rounded stones beneath my bare feet, smooth after countless centuries of cascade. *I'm somewhere different, am I not?*

A place between the centuries, a place where I could catch my breath.

Finally, a home?

I turned a bit, and the rain rotated as well, this sea salt rain, as gray as the rocky ground. My cloak of rain. However, I also felt the nourishing power, understood that the slash and run of the water circulated back upward, that there were no clouds, no stars above, just looping currents for me alone to ford. The air was heavy, mineral. I cupped my hands and drank what I thought would be the water of knowledge and found it startlingly bland, lifeless. The salt it contained seemed exhausted of nutrition. It tasted like how some journeys end.

But of course, time contains no life. It is but a crumbling road, a looping Appian Way littered with graves. Then the water stopped falling all at once, and the final splash erupted into a fog that curled in on itself, effervescent and everywhere convulsing grayness with slight pirouettes that quivered and beckoned. Soon this parted to reveal a sudden wall rising from the path. Then the inevitable door within the wall appeared. I opened it and stepped inside.

But it looked so different. Of course, the cataracts of thirst had been washed away, and for the first time, I could see the Baths of Caracalla for the palace of wisdom it was.

What marvelous halls. The marble just polished, the gleam of sunlight off the floor was striking, with additional starlight captured and stored in the cornices to illuminate midnight discoveries. The columns hung majestic, upholding a place of peace and contemplation. There were a few others here, but everyone seemed to be at a distance, lost in their own contemplation. My nakedness went unnoticed as I strolled familiar yet alien corridors. The double doors I remembered so well swung open onto a large library. The shelves held the philosophies and poetry of generations, past and future. Maybe it was time to reread Lucretius, Hesiod, Ovid. I knew where all my favorites were, and this time each page would be a lush honeycomb of words, ideas, truths to be rediscovered.

I pulled down a scroll and unfurled its wings of poetry and understanding. After hours of reading and losing myself in clouds of script and ink, I took a soak in the *tepidarium* and let the heat tickle my feet. Perhaps I will find a man, but my mind is on the kind merchant Odoacer, forever smiling, bald and squinting within his reliable poolside booth. He sells the most exquisite stylus and fine Egyptian papyrus to boot. It is high time I tell my story. From the pool's edge, as my feet dangle above placid waters, I can see the bluest sky, and can see that for now, the sun will never set.

Moreover, when said stylus starts to run dry, a knowing flick of my tongue will certainly excite a hitherto unknown reserve of the whitest, most pure and milky ink.

Surely, I will like the taste.

POSTSCRIPT

A Note to Readers and Recommended Readings

I wish I could tell you an additional tale of scholarly research, of hours poring over rare texts late at night in prestigious libraries. However, it is probably better that I apologize to any randy academic or armchair archeologist who raised an eyebrow now and again at wild inaccuracies or historical liberties that rubbed them the wrong way. Or maybe not. After all, my challenge here was to run through an erotic journey, not teach class. My love for and fascination with the classical world has been one of the most enduring relationships in my literary life as both reader and writer. It has never been a marriage, however, but rather an affair conducted on the fly.

This all started my last semester of graduate school. I had put off the required classics course until the very end—and it blew me away. From Homer to Virgil to Tacitus, I was hooked. Tacitus, in particular, struck a chord. *The Annals of Imperial Rome* presented a parallel world that is also the progenitor of our Western reality. It quickly joined my list of favorite books, which at the time was mostly novels. Now that I read mostly nonfiction, I look back and wonder if this was one of those books on which the crux of such a big change turned? Every used bookstore, which I had previously haunted for obscure science fiction and fantasy titles, suddenly opened up to an unknown attic of ancient history.

I devoured these texts for about a decade, filling my shelves with cracked and mottled Penguin Classics bookended by brittle copies of Loeb Classical Library editions. I also absorbed fiction concerning the era. Robert Graves, of course, but also less obvious work, like John Hersey's epistolary novel about an attempted assignation of Nero, *The Conspiracy* (that, so many years later, influenced my story, "The Love of the Emperor Is Divine," found in my second short story collection, *Night Sweats: Tales of Homosexual Wonder and Woe*). Coming out of the closet switched my attention to all books gay, and the titillation of so much bawdy, off-the-cuff gay sex found in Roman writing was definitely an important step for me in that direction. Still, I read a novel or nonfiction book of the Roman Empire each year: the biography of an emperor that challenges preconceived notions, or a book on ancient architecture. Really, whatever strikes my fancy. And not necessarily a new book. The discovery of something out of print or off-kilter has a special allure.

Let me take this moment to recommend a title from our Most Imminent Mother Superior, Gore Vidal. His novel *Julian*, about the last pagan ruler of Rome (and post-Constantine at that), is an absolutely fantastic read. One of the very few books I have read twice. I don't recall any specific gay content, though the death of paganism kind of covers that, eh?

❖

The thing with *The Lurid Sea* is that I'd told the story to friends several times over dinner or drinks when answering the question, "So, what are you working on?" And now I needed to capture it on paper, this being the first book I wrote under a contractual deadline. I decided that erotic energy would carry the story to the date in question, that research would mean a lot of digressive reading, and that I would be chasing historical accuracy rather than steamy necessity. Not that I couldn't have done both, but that's when you spend years on a writing project, and I have convinced myself to write fast as a way of actually staying alive. It's how I breathe. I have always been influenced by the (hopefully not apocryphal) story that Anthony Burgess wrote *A Clockwork Orange* and maybe two other books—including possibly *The Wanting Seed*—thinking he had a deadly cancer (he had been misdiagnosed) and wanted to leave something behind to generate royalties for his then young family. So I was halfway through the manuscript, with all the major points plotted out (mostly fill-in-the-blank writing, which is the most fun until you are down to the last two blanks, as no one saves the easiest stuff for last) when I decided to do some minor research. I wanted to confirm some hunches on Roman sexuality and basically just check in with an era that had captivated me for the entirety of my adulthood.

I instinctively knew from my readings that the Romans did not suffer our current rigid dichotomy when it came to sexuality, so I picked up the now indispensible *Roman Homosexuality: Second Edition*, by Craig A. Williams (Oxford University Press). I can't recommend this book enough. Obviously, it was useful informing the context of all the fuckery I was creating, but the absolute wealth of source material made reading it the literary equivalent of discovering Pompeii. Additionally, after starting *The Lurid Sea*, I became aware of the Japanese manga *Thermae Romae*. I knew this comic book contained a time travel element dealing with a bathhouse in ancient Rome as well as a modern Japanese one. Since I did not detect any gay content—and I absolutely love and collect gay Japanese comics—I didn't pay it much attention other than to post it on the Roman mystery writer Steve Saylor's Facebook page, where he absolutely flipped, not having previously known about it. Fun fact: he is the pseudonymous author of *Slaves of the Empire*, a totally hot, brutal gay gladiator romp, published under the name Aaron Travis. Then, while in Japan on vacation, editing *The Lurid Sea* most mornings over coffee, I was surprised to discover that Netflix changes content in other countries, and I found the film version of *Thermae Romae*. It is a fun flick, and its lead actor is a hottie.

Of equal influence to the historical antecedents are the erotic books that absolutely turned me on. First and foremost, Samuel R. Delany's *Hogg* grabbed me by the horns. In terms of strict erotic writing, I have found the opening chapters to be a constant go-to when I'm looking to get off. As much as I am attracted, in reading as well as writing, to exploring the meanings and permutations of extreme violence, I have yet to finish *Hogg*. I find the rest of the book just so disturbing. What I have completed, over and over, are several of the collected works of Boyd McDonald. His *Straight to Hell* chapbooks were formative texts in my commitment to sexual honesty. Early on, one of my first lovers kept all of his gay contraband stuffed into a rather ridiculous-looking red suitcase under his bed. It was a treasure chest for me. Slippery dildoes and other implements aside, I still have the two volumes of Boyd McDonald's *Straight to Hell* series, *Lewd* and *Scum*, stored within, gifted to me when he downsized apartments. Bibles both. McDonald led a monastic life in an SRO compiling erotic compendiums in the '70s and '80s, with men from all over the world mailing him their sexual confessions: raw moments that had never before been so publicly revealed. He made physical truths accessible, valid.

This book is dedicated to Boyd McDonald.

Another important window into gay bathhouse culture,

serving as both a work of art and a historical document, is Michael Rumaker's 1979 book, *A Day and Night at the Baths*. This autobiographical account of his visit to the infamous Everard Baths in Manhattan (nicknamed "Ever Hard" back in the day by cheeky New Yorkers in the know—the same bathhouse featured in Andrew Holleran's classic *Dancer From the Dance*) is a brilliant poetic letter in a bottle, preserving a moment in gay culture while expounding on the psychological and sociological beats entering such spaces meant to gay men at that time (and now as well, depending on where you live). I was fortunate enough to be invited by William Johnson, the editor of *Mary: A Literary Quarterly*, to interview Michael about the formation of his book, then coming back into print. Highly recommended for readers who crave even more steamy journeys.

Additional influences: as I was making my way into the world of gay letters and getting published for the first time, I was fortunate enough to be introduced to Wayne Courtois's *My Name Is Rand*, a genuine new classic of erotica, an intense tale of kidnapping and tickle torture. For a fledgling writer, it was an important lesson in how to follow an extreme idea to its natural conclusion in a satisfactory manner. We became buddies, and he blurbed my first published book, appropriately enough an erotic novel, *The Werewolves of Central Park*. I am also glad I read John Rechy early on. I happened to have devoured *City of Night* while on my own tour of New York City's nocturnal piers and weird video stores, so it was an organic, timely read. Whenever I was hungover, marking out foggy, next-day scratches in spiraled books, I felt like a novice comparing notes with the master. I also thoroughly enjoyed the heightened immediacy of his novel *Rushes*—reminiscent of *A Day and a Night at the Baths* in how it takes place in real time, but it is a much starker book, if memory serves.

In getting to know some of the writers I was reading and finding that many of the books they were recommending were out of print, I took it upon myself to edit a collection of essays along this topic: *The Lost Library: Gay Fiction Rediscovered*. I asked writers I either knew or was reading to pitch in and to invite compatriots. Wayne contributed a piece, and of course several of the titles dealt directly with bathhouses. One of my good friends from the Velvet Mafia (an online magazine of gay fiction and reviews, very left-of-center, down-and-dirty, and importantly, just plain fun), Ian Titus, wrote about *Vanishing Rooms* by Melvin Dixon. The book features fantastic scenes in the Paradise Baths, likely an amalgamation of several Manhattan saunas and sex clubs. Unfortunately, *Vanishing Rooms* has slipped back out of print after surfacing again in the early 2000s. It is unlikely that *Saul's Book*, by Paul T. Rogers, reviewed by Paul Russell, will see the light of day again. Rogers was brutally murdered shortly after its publication by the lover he attempted to immortalize in said book, one that runs the gamut of Times Square sex clubs and bathhouses. Another gem I was introduced to in assembling *The Lost Library* was *Child of the Sun*. Reviewed by gay literary historian Michael Bronski, this randy novel about the Emperor Heliogabalus was a fun, pulpy read. The authors, Kyle Onstott, known for writing *Mandingo*, and Lance Horner, deliver a campy, fictionalized version of the young gay emperor, complete with gay marriage and a shameless approach to smut.

Not every out-of-print gay book that crossed my path made it into *The Lost Library*. One that I wished someone had covered was Jay B. Laws's *Steam*. An AIDS horror novel written and published during the darkest days of the plague, a bathhouse is central to its dark action. As with many gay writers taken too soon, very little information about him is available. You could say the same thing about the multitude of bathhouses shuttered during the plague years. Even now, our stories remain on the margin, ephemeral. One corrective is the documentary *Continental,* about the Continental Baths and its important role in gay sexual liberation during the early '70s. I attended a screening at the Brooklyn Academy of Music, and it was wonderful to have the story of this iconographic venue shown in a large theater before a rapt, appreciative audience, with many of the players present to take questions after the film.

So this postscript turned out to be overlong, and probably of interest to only a few, but if you're like me, talking about books can be almost as fun as reading them—and certainly writing them. I certainly enjoyed imagining and then writing *this* book, as well as sharing a bit of the backstory with you here. Notice that I didn't mention anything about the in-person research. That's a story for another day, another book, perhaps.

Or maybe I'll just write Boyd a letter.

About the Author

Tom Cardamone is the author of the Lambda Literary Award–winning speculative novella *Green Thumb* and the erotic fantasy novel *The Werewolves of Central Park* as well as the novella *Pacific Rimming*. His short story collection, *Pumpkin Teeth*, was a finalist for the Lambda Literary Award and Black Quill Award.

He has edited *The Lost Library: Gay Fiction Rediscovered* and the anthology *Lavender Menace: Tales of Queer Villainy!*, which was nominated for the Over The Rainbow List by the LGBT Round Table of the American Library Association.

Lambda Literary Review described his 2016 collection, *Night Sweats: Tales of Homosexual Wonder and Woe*, as "a heady mix of subtle, understated wonder, unmitigated horror, and powerful eroticism, with each story working its individual magic on the reader."

Books Available From Bold Strokes Books

The Lurid Sea by Tom Cardamone. Cursed to spend eternity on his knees, Nerites is having the time of his life. (978-1-62639-911-2)

Sinister Justice by Steve Pickens. When a vigilante targets citizens of Jake Finnigan's hometown, Jake and his partner Sam fall under suspicion themselves as they investigate the murders. (978-1-63555-094-8)

Club Arcana: Operation Janus by Jon Wilson. Wizards, demons, Elder Gods: Who knew the universe was so crowded, and that they'd all be out to get Angus McAslan? (978-1-62639-969-3)

Triad Soul by 'Nathan Burgoine. Luc, Anders, and Curtis—vampire, demon, and wizard—must use their powers of blood, soul, and magic to defeat a murderer determined to turn their city into a battlefield. (978-1-62639-863-4)

Gatecrasher by Stephen Graham King. Aided by a high-tech thief, the Maverick Heart crew race against time to prevent a cadre of savage corporate mercenaries from seizing control of a revolutionary wormhole technology. (978-1-62639-936-5)

Wicked Frat Boy Ways by Todd Gregory. Beta Kappa brothers Brandon Benson and Phil Connor play an increasingly dangerous game of love, seduction, and emotional manipulation. (978-1-62639-671-5)

Death Goes Overboard by David S. Pederson. Heath Barrington and Alan Keyes are two sides of a steamy love triangle as they encounter gangsters, con men, murder, and more aboard an old lake steamer. (978-1-62639-907-5)

A Careful Heart by Ralph Josiah Bardsley. Be careful what you wish for…love changes everything. (978-1-62639-887-0)

Worms of Sin by Lyle Blake Smythers. A haunted mental asylum turned drug treatment facility exposes supernatural detective Finn M'Coul to an outbreak of murderous insanity, a strange parasite, and ghosts that seek sex with the living. (978-1-62639-823-8)

Tartarus by Eric Andrews-Katz. When Echidna, Mother of all Monsters, escapes from Tartarus and into the modern world, only an Olympian has the power to oppose her. (978-1-62639-746-0)

Rank by Richard Compson Sater. Rank means nothing to the heart, but the Air Force isn't as impartial. Every airman learns that rank has its privileges. What about love? (978-1-62639-845-0)

The Grim Reaper's Calling Card by Donald Webb. When Katsuro Tanaka begins investigating the disappearance of a young nurse, he discovers more missing persons, and they all have one thing in common: The Grim Reaper Tarot Card. (978-1-62639-748-4)

Smoldering Desires by C.E. Knipes. Evan McGarrity has found the man of his dreams in Sebastian Tantalos. When an old boyfriend from Sebastian's past enters the picture, Evan must fight for the man he loves. (978-1-62639-714-9)

Tallulah Bankhead Slept Here by Sam Lollar. A coming of age/coming out story, set in El Paso of 1967, that tells of Aaron's adventures with movie stars, cool cars, and topless bars. (978-1-62639-710-1)

Death Came Calling by Donald Webb. When private investigator Katsuro Tanaka is hired to look into the death of a high-profile lawyer, he becomes embroiled in a case of murder and mayhem. (978-1-60282-979-4)

The City of Seven Gods by Andrew J. Peters. In an ancient city of aerie temples, a young priest and a barbarian mercenary struggle to refashion their lives after their worlds are torn apart by betrayal. (978-1-62639-775-0)

Lysistrata Cove by Dena Hankins. Jack and Eve navigate the maelstrom of their darkest desires and find love by transgressing gender, dominance, submission, and the law on the crystal blue Caribbean Sea. (978-1-62639-821-4)

Garden District Gothic by Greg Herren. Scotty Bradley has to solve a notorious thirty-year-old unsolved murder that has terrible repercussions in the present. (978-1-62639-667-8)

The Man on Top of the World by Vanessa Clark. Jonathan Maxwell falling in love with Izzy Rich, the world's hottest glam rock superstar, is not only unpredictable but complicated when a bold teenage fan-girl changes everything. (978-1-62639-699-9)

The Orchard of Flesh by Christian Baines. With two hotheaded men under his roof including his werewolf lover, a vampire tries to solve an increasingly lethal mystery while keeping Sydney's supernatural factions from the brink of war. (978-1-62639-649-4)

Funny Bone by Daniel W. Kelly. Sometimes sex feels so good you just gotta giggle! (978-1-62639-683-8)

The Thassos Confabulation by Sam Sommer. With the inheritance of a great deal of money, David and Chris also inherit a nondescript brown paper parcel and a strange and perplexing letter that sends David on a quest to understand its meaning. (978-1-62639-665-4)

The Photographer's Truth by Ralph Josiah Bardsley. Silicon Valley tech geek Ian Baines gets more than he bargained for on an unexpected journey of self-discovery through the lustrous nightlife of Paris. (978-1-62639-637-1)

Crimson Souls by William Holden. A scorned shadow demon brings a centuries-old vendetta to a bloody end as he assembles the last of the descendants of Harvard's Secret Court. (978-1-62639-628-9)

boldstrokesbooks.com

Bold Strokes Books

Quality and Diversity in LGBTQ Literature

victory
EDITIONS

Drama

MATINEE BOOKS

SCI-FI

E-BOOKS

MYSTERY

HE
erotica

EROTICA

BSB
SOLILOQUY

YOUNG ADULT

BS
BOLD
STROKES
BOOKS

LIBERTY
EDITION

Romance

W·E·B·S·T·O·R·E

PRINT AND EBOOKS